D1525072

# Smart
# Alex

SAM CHEEVER

~SC~

**In the twisted mind of a clever killer, her intelligence makes her a prize worth taking. By whatever means.**

Matthew Smart has lost his Assistant, Cameron, in a brutal killing. Devastated, Matthew has to find out who murdered his employee while interviewing potential replacements. Strangely, the applicants all seem to be blowing off their interviews. So when a bold, softly curved beauty named Alexis McFadden shows up in his office looking to fill the position, he's tempted to hire her just because she's the only one who wants the job, although he doesn't believe she's a good fit. Lucky for Alex, a tricky new case convinces Matthew that he can really use her help. But what if Alex is smart enough to get herself hired against all odds, while in the eyes of a cold-blooded killer, she's too smart by half?

# CHAPTER ONE

It wasn't the constant barking that ripped nails across his nerves when he opened the door. Or even the growl that followed on its tail. It was the deep, unnatural silence accompanied by a butcher store smell.

Matthew Smart grabbed his Glock nine millimeter from his waistband and shushed his dog. "Sit, Max."

The tiny dachshund did as he was told, dropping to his quivering buttocks on the hard-wood floor. But the growl vibrating in his throat didn't soften. If anything it grew.

Matthew gave the room a quick look, ducking into the small restroom his clients used, and returned to the office where his assistant, Cameron should have been typing up Matthew's notes from the day before.

No Cameron. No typing. And then there was that smell...

Max was up again, his tail wagging high and fast, a key to his aggressive mood. In case Matthew missed the constant growling.

Matthew crept along the wall dividing the outer office from his inner sanctuary. His hands tightened around his Glock. His office door was open a few inches. It had been closed and locked the night before when he'd left.

SAM CHEEVER

The frosted glass in the door was splattered with something that had dried in trails down the glass. Matthew's nose twitched as he pushed on the door with his fingertips, hanging back as it creaked slowly open. The elderly ceiling fan above his desk spun lazily overhead, giving off a soft click with each rotation.

On the rug in front of the door was a mug. The contents of the mug formed a black stain on Matthew's inexpensive Oriental rug, painting jagged stripes over the interior of the door. A manila folder, its guts spread across the rug alongside the spilled coffee, explained why the door was unlocked.

Matthew's office was empty. But his gaze slipped quickly over the chaos that had once been his refuge. The place had been tossed.

Max trotted through the door and Matthew started to call him back. But the little dog didn't go far. He sniffed the spilled coffee, dancing sideways through the detritus of Matthew's professional life lying broken and disheveled over the floor. Max's short fringe of a tail whipped the air. His moist black nostrils flared over the scattered papers, scenting them. He whined plaintively.

Matthew's boots crunched over broken glass as he made a quick circuit of the office, finding it just as empty as the outer office had been.

"Come on, Max." There was one more room to search. Matthew's palms were damp on the Glock as he moved back through the outer office, heading toward the closed door on the back wall of the main room. He turned the knob with his fingertips, taking care not to touch the back of the knob where, if he was really lucky, he'd be able to pull a fingerprint or two later.

The door stuck, swollen in its frame, and Matthew had to put his shoulder into it to wrench it open. The stench that had greeted him when he'd entered Smart Investigations, Inc. punched him hard once the supply room door was open. He staggered back a step, his stomach roiling.

Max gave a chirp of warning and Matthew lifted his Glock to chest height, allowing it to precede him into the long, narrow room.

A moment later he lowered it again, swearing.

The room was empty except for the man sitting in the desk chair that should have been behind Cameron's desk. Purple faced with eyes bulging and several long bloody gashes decorating his arms and legs, the man was clearly dead. He wouldn't be attacking anybody. And whoever had tied the long scarf around his throat and spun the desk chair until he choked to death was already gone.

Max gave a single bark and ran over to lick the tips of Cameron's long fingers. The little dog's tail wagged in greeting for a beat and then drooped. He dropped to his haunches and gave a plaintive whine, finally turning to look a question at Matthew.

Matthew scrubbed a hand over his jaw, his eyes filling with tears. "Aw, Cam. Who the hell did this to you?"

~SC~

Alexis McFadden stared down the little man giving her snake eye across the room. "I can't believe you're firing me."

The little twerp smiled meanly. "Your work was sub-par. I'm giving you a whole week's pay as severance, McFadden. You have nothing to complain about."

She snorted, taking a step closer. He cringed back, his hands coming up to fend her off. She almost smiled. Alex wasn't afraid to use her size to intimidate when she thought it was justified. "Nothing, huh? You're firing me because I thought receiving a text picture of your junk in stained underwear was outside my job description? Is that what you mean by sub-par?"

The little man shrugged. "You're delusional. I can't help it if you have a quirky admirer. The junk in that picture wasn't mine and you can't prove it was."

Unfortunately the cagey little bastard wasn't wrong. And that was what was making Alex crazy. He'd used a burner phone to send her the disgusting pictures. Just in case she didn't take it well. She almost laughed at the thought.

Like anybody would take that well.

"You're right, it could have just been somebody's little pinkie finger stuffed into the front of his undies."

The smug grin slid away. "Get the hell out of here, McFadden. You're fired. And you can forget that week of severance."

She shook her head, flinging the files she'd carried into his office onto his desk. "It's a shame, I could have used that dollar fifty to buy a candy bar or something."

She strode out of the office and headed for the door, determined not to look back. The job had been underwhelming anyway and the man who'd hired her was a perv of the highest order. She'd been shaking off his advances for weeks. If she hadn't really needed the money…

And that reminder made her sigh. She really did need the job, not to mention the work. Sitting around her studio apartment thinking about everything that had recently gone wrong in her life wasn't doing a thing for her already acerbic personality.

The sun climbed out of the clouds long enough to warm the top of her head as Alex stepped outside, descending the rust-stained concrete steps to the sidewalk. A moist breeze filtered past, ruffling her heavy, mahogany-brown hair. The air promised rain, reminding her that the weather dude had predicted storms. Even as she had the thought another draft, stronger and cooler, blew her dress around her thighs.

A sharp tone brought Alex's head up. The man who'd whistled doffed a hard hat and wagged his tongue at her. She rolled her eyes, shaking her head, and pulled the thin sweater she'd donned that morning closer. Thunder rolled across the sky and, just before Alex ducked into the parking garage, the first fat drops of rain pinged against her face.

Just great. The wipers on her ancient beetle bug had stopped working days earlier and she didn't have the money to get them fixed. She'd have to start looking for another job right away. Hopefully one that was better suited to her skill set. One with a female boss, she decided as she pulled the door of her little blue rust bucket open and ducked inside. She was really tired of dealing with men who thought the world revolved around them and their tiny little penises.

In fact, she was just plain tired of dealing with men. She'd be fine if she didn't have to talk to one again for at least a month. Maybe a year.

~SC~

The glass in the windows rattled as another blast of wind shoved against the building. Raindrops hit the roof of the old, brick structure so hard Matthew thought there might be hail. He stood in front of the window, watching a tiny blue car creep down the street, a pale hand occasionally reaching through the open window and swiping across the splintered windshield before a burst of speed and then a repeat of the process. He shook his head. Somebody needed a new car.

"Any idea who could have done this to your assistant?"

Matthew turned to look at Detective Hanks, a slender woman with piercing brown eyes and lips that seemed always to have just sucked a lemon. He shook his head. "No idea. But I'm going to find out."

She lowered delicate blonde brows at him. "Matt…"

"Matthew. Please. A mat is something you wipe your feet on."

She stared at him a long moment, her gaze like pincers trying to pry open his scalp to see inside. "You need to leave this to the police."

He nodded. "You got it."

The lemon lips pursed tighter, until they resembled somebody's anus. "You're just humoring me aren't you?"

"Yes. I am." He turned away from the window and fixed her with a sincere look. Well, it was as sincere as he could make it given the fact that it was totally not sincere. "I promise I'll stay out of your way and I won't do anything to compromise your investigation."

She shook her head, clearly not believing him. There was a reason Cindy Hanks was a detective. She could read people like a thousand dollar a hand poker player. "I really hate it when you lie to my face, Matt."

He didn't take the bait again, knowing he deserved the jab. "I gave you my most sincere manner and you repay me by butchering my name?"

She finally laughed. "You're incorrigible."

"I try. But seriously, Cindy. I want to find this guy even more than you do. Whatever he might have done, Cameron didn't deserve this."

"Have you considered the possibility that this wasn't about Cam?"

Matthew had thought of that. In fact he'd thought of little else since finding the body. "You're thinking it was Bigg."

"Patrick Bigg didn't take kindly to your arresting his son. This…" She swept her hand toward the storage room, where an empty chair sat in the center of the long room, "would fit nicely with Bigg's world view about an eye for an eye."

Matthew bit back a sharp retort. After all, he'd hardly tortured Mika Bigg slowly to death. He'd simply caught him with his well-manicured fingers in the wrong piggy bank and gotten him a one-way ticket to maximum security in Michigan City, Indiana. "You're right. I think you should check that out."

She cocked her head. "You want me to check on Bigg? Why are you being so reasonable?"

"I'm not stupid, Cindy. I'm like a match to Bigg's dynamite right now. You'll get much further with him than I would."

"In other words, you don't believe he's our guy?"

"No. I don't. Bigg would deal directly with me. He doesn't believe in sending messages. He's not that subtle."

"You could be right. I'll speak to him. But I tend to agree." She fixed him with a look. "You really need to stay away from this investigation, Matthew. Let me do my job."

"I can't do that. Cameron was one of mine. He was under my protection. I'm going to find out what happened here and make sure somebody pays." He lifted an eyebrow. "This is what I do, Cin. Have you forgotten?"

"No. But you're too close to this one. Too emotional."

"Emotions are what make me good at what I do. I care about all of my clients. That's why I work so hard to help them."

Shaking her head, she headed for the door. "I'll let you know what forensics finds. If we're lucky we'll find a print on the tape bindings or DNA on the scarf."

Matthew nodded. "Thanks, Cin." He turned back to the window as the detective cleared out, leaving him to his thoughts. Matthew wasn't going to start with Patrick Bigg and his dirty organization. He was going to start a lot closer to home. It was clear Cameron had been tortured for information on something. While it was possible the killer had been looking for information on one of Matthew's cases, it seemed more likely he would have picked on Matthew rather than Cameron for that.

Unless he'd seen Matthew's military records. He'd held out five more seconds during the water boarding portion of training than anyone else in the S.E.R.E. survival course he'd undergone in the Navy. Anyone who knew that would see Cameron as the weaker link for getting information. But it was highly unlikely anybody but another Navy Seal would know about the stat. Anything for public consumption was heavily redacted. Everything they did was eyes only and the pool of eyes that would have had access was extremely small.

No. Matthew thought whoever killed Cameron was looking for something either Cameron had or believed Cameron's death would soften Matthew up for something. Either way, Matthew was going to put a spike in the heart of the killer's plans.

He wouldn't rest until he'd found the guy and brought him to justice.

# CHAPTER TWO

Alex printed the job lead for a personal assistant at Smart Investigations, Inc and put it on the pile with the others. The job would be perfect for her skill set. She'd always been fascinated by the whole idea of investigating stuff and she could safely use her genius level IQ finding bad guys for her hapless new boss.

Grinning widely, she berated herself for being overconfident but the job was the first one she'd found in days that she considered even mildly interesting. And M. Smart, no doubt a woman because only women used first initials, was about to become the recipient of a full scale Alex charm offensive—hopefully light on the offensive part. Though Alex's determination had been known to terrify the faint of heart.

Alex pulled up her resume and started rewriting it to include the keywords from the job ad. She reworked the tasks from her previous jobs to highlight problem solving and security strengths. And she fleshed out her brief stint as a night security guard at a large discount store warehouse. Then she took her picture off the resume and changed Alexis to Alex. Two could play at the pretend name game. Let the other woman be just as surprised as

Alex would pretend to be over the sex of her new employee.

After another hour of tweaking and perfecting, Alex took a deep breath, her finger hovering over the Enter key, and then sent the resume into the cyber void. She forced herself to rise from her chair and leave the apartment. A nice, long run should clear her head and settle her nerves. Hopefully softening the fear that she'd be rejected for the job before she got the chance to charm her new boss into offering it to her.

~SC~

Scratching Max's softly furred back; Matthew opened the latest resume and quickly scanned it. He frowned, wondering why on earth a guy who'd gotten a 4.0 at Kelley School of Business IU would bother with a measly assistant's job at a private investigator's office. He printed the resume and slid it to the bottom of a quickly dwindling pile. When he'd started the search for the perfect…and then a good…and then a serviceable…and finally a competent assistant, he'd had no idea how hard it would prove to be. He'd spent hours of every day for the last week trying to find somebody. But every time he made an appointment the applicant either didn't show or had an accident on the way to the interview. If it wasn't the wrong time of year, Matthew would think that Mercury was in retrograde again. He'd never had such bad luck interviewing assistants. When he'd hired Cameron it had taken him just four interviews and he'd worked happily with the other man for five productive years.

Thoughts of Cameron made Matthew frown. Once he recovered from the stifling melancholy brought on by Cam's death, Matthew had been so busy trying to replace his assistant that he hadn't had time to dig too deeply into Cam's murder. Despite his sadness, Matthew had to hire somebody soon so he could focus on the case. Though he wondered if the dozen or so applications currently lining the bottom of his trash can were signs of his reluctance to replace a man who'd become as much a friend as an assistant.

His cell phone rang and he hit Answer without looking at the number. "Smart."

"Yes I am and so is my brother."

Matthew smiled. "And your other brothers too?"

Brandon Smart chuckled. "Yeah. Them too. But none of them are nearly as smart as my sister." Matthew's brother hesitated a moment and when he spoke again the smile was missing from his voice. "How you doin', little bro?"

"Just exactly as well as the last time you asked me…this morning I think."

Brandon smiled. He took his job as the oldest of five siblings very seriously. "Sorry. Since you yelled at Wally and Butch the family made me the designated emotional health checker."

"Lucky you."

"Yeah. Something was said about my skin being thicker than T-Rex hide."

"Well you can report to one and all that I'm doing fine. In fact I've started to look for Cam's replacement."

"Ugh. How's that going?"

Matthew glanced at his watch, realizing that his interview was late. Really late. Expelling a frustrated breath, he had to admit to himself that he'd been stood up again. "Not so good. I'm starting to think there's nobody left with a work ethic."

"Tandy will come down and help. You know she loves doing it."

Matthew grimaced. The youngest Smart and only female sibling did love being in Matthew's office and pretending to be an investigator, but she was really more interested in the girly suits and high heels she got to wear and less interested in doing any actual work. "If I get really desperate I'll let you know. I've gotta go."

"Okay. I'll talk to you in…" Matthew could picture his brother glancing at his watch. "About fourteen hours. That should give you plenty of time to prep for your next report to your loving if slightly intrusive family unit."

"I'll save you a call. I'm fine. You can report to them I'll be fine in the morning and tomorrow night and the next morning…"

"Nice try, bro. Talk to you in the morning."

Shaking his head, Matthew disconnected and pulled the resume for the latest no-show off the top of the pile, throwing it into the trash. Picking up his cell phone, Matthew started to dial the next applicant's phone number. The papers on his desk fluttered and Max growled softly, rising to his feet inside the tiny bed atop Matthew's desk. Then he stilled, cocking his head, and his fringe of a tail swiped the air happily as he bunched to jump to the floor.

"Hold on there, hot shot." Matthew scooped him up and settled him to the floor just as the outside door closed and a woman's voice called out from the front office.

"Hello? Is anybody here?"

Max shot through the door, tail wagging happily.

Matthew followed the sound of giggling to the outer office, where he found, to his amazement, Max wriggling happily in a gorgeous woman's arms, enthusiastically licking her face.

He frowned, unused to his dog taking so quickly to another person. "Can I help you?"

The woman's gaze slid to him and Matthew felt something catch in the center of his chest. Her wide, gray-blue eyes were tilted up slightly on the outside corners, giving her a decidedly exotic look. The stunning gaze was made even more beautiful by the thick fan of lashes rimming it. She looked to be about five ten, very curvy, and when she smiled at him over Max's traitorous little face, twin dimples appeared on her cheeks.

A jolt of pure sexual awareness speared through him and Matthew nearly forgot to breathe under its power.

"Hi. I'm sorry to bother you," she said.

Not exactly a full explanation of her presence in his outer office, but Matthew barely noticed. He let his gaze slide over her, noting the running shoes and the well-washed sweatpants that complemented rather than hid her long, long legs. The long-sleeved gray tee shirt she wore hugged her full breasts lovingly and tucked into her waist before flaring out over well-rounded hips. She wore her thick mahogany hair pulled back in a ponytail that swung in a silky wave when she twisted away from Max's loving kiss a moment later.

She definitely wasn't a client. Not dressed like that. He hoped she wasn't his next interview. Aside from being seriously underdressed, that would make her either an hour late for her appointment or a couple of hours early. Besides, her effect on him was troubling to say the least. He hadn't had such a strong reaction to a woman in years.

The woman finally placed Max on the ground, patting his head as he hopped around her in blatant adoration. "I'm so sorry." She wiped her hand over her sweatpants. "I'm Alex. Alex McFadden."

The name was familiar but Matthew couldn't quite grasp where he'd seen it before. He shook her hand, noting both the exquisite softness and strength of her grip. "Matthew Smart." He nodded toward his traitorous partner. "That's Max. He's human resources."

She narrowed her gaze in confusion.

"He's an exceptional judge of character. I won't hire anyone he doesn't like," Matthew clarified, frowning. "He really seems to like you."

She lifted her hands out to her sides and cocked her head, grinning. "What's not to like?"

Matthew laughed, enjoying the way her dimples flashed when she joined him. "I like a person with confidence."

She shook her head. "What you're mistaking for confidence is really a deep sense of discomfort with self, tinged with a need for approval that causes me to resort to self-deprecation and humor to compensate."

He just blinked, unsure how to respond.

She sighed. "And an annoying tendency to overshare." She looked around the office as if judging its acceptance. After a moment she gave a single nod. "I approve."

Matthew was torn between the fact that he couldn't help liking her and the equally unsettling fact that he had no idea who she was. "Ms. McFadden…"

"Alex. Please." She cast her startling gaze over him. "So you're M. Smart. Good thing your first initial isn't I."

He chuckled. "That would just be bragging."

"I'm just curious. Why the initial? Usually only women do that, to hide the fact that they're female so they won't be prejudged."

Matthew shrugged. "I hate it when people call me Matt. If I send my name into cyberspace it always comes back as Matt."

She nodded. "I can respect that. I'm just the opposite. I prefer Alex to Alexis."

"Understood." Unfortunately, that was all he understood. "Ms…Alex…"

"You might as well know right up front that I tend to do and say what I think without a lot of filters."

He nodded. "Okay."

"I'm also a rescuer." When he gave her a blank look she explained. "I rescue small animals and stuff. Sometimes people." She shrugged.

"Ah. No wonder Max likes you."

"He likes me because I told him he's handsome."

Matthew felt his eyes going wide.

She laughed. "I was just tweaking you about that. I mean, I did tell him he was handsome, but I don't really believe he understood me. He understood my tone of voice of course, which said, you are so dang cute I just want to snuggle you tight. But he didn't understand the words. Dogs don't speak human."

Matthew wasn't so sure about that. Max certainly

understood the words ice cream and car ride. "Ms…Alex, I'm sorry. Did we have an appointment?"

She stared at him for a moment and then slapped herself on the forehead. "Oh god. I'm so sorry. Not yet. I mean. I just sent you my resume and went out for a run. And then I realized your office was a few blocks away from my apartment and before I knew it I was running this way. I just wanted to introduce myself. You know, put a face with the resume. And to tell you I'd really like the job."

Matthew finally realized why he recognized her name. She was the last resume he'd received. The Alex he'd assumed was a guy. Overqualified. "Oh. I see. Well it's a pleasure to meet you, Alex…"

Her smile slid away and he felt its loss like a kick in the gut. "You've hired someone already."

"Um. No. Not yet."

The dimples returned. "Oh, good. Then I'm not too late."

"But…"

The dimples disappeared.

"I'm afraid you're way overqualified for the position."

"I don't mind. I have some ideas for how I can be more help to you. I'm really good at puzzle solving. Maybe I can help with your investigations."

Matthew shook his head. "I'm sorry."

The outer door opened and a man stood there, looking from one to the other of them. His long, ruddy face was fixed in an angry frown. Heavy brown eyebrows, slightly darker than the military-short hair on his head, lowered over smallish blue eyes. He was a big guy, over six feet tall, and looked to be in his mid-fifties. The man nodded at Alex and then turned to Matthew, dismissing her.

Max growled softly.

"I'm looking for Matthew Smart."

Matthew stepped forward, taking the man's hand. "I'm Matthew Smart."

The other man tugged on his ear and looked down at his feet. "I'm John Snow. I want to hire you to find the person who killed my daughter."

~SC~

Of course Alex didn't miss the way John Snow dismissed her. She had a long history of experience with men who saw a pretty, buxom woman and figured she had nothing between her ears but bubbles. However, she didn't mind the fact that John Snow had apparently forgotten she was there. She used the opportunity to study him. To assess his mannerisms, read his body language. She was uncomfortable with what she saw. Flashing Matthew a glance, she noted the slight tightening around his lips that told her he probably felt the same way. In that moment, Alex knew Matthew Smart was undoubtedly very good at his job. A worthy partner. She determined to get the job as his assistant no matter what it took.

"Please, come into my office, Mr. Snow." Matthew indicated the door he'd exited to greet her a few minutes earlier. John Snow inclined his head and moved toward the door. Max was close on his heels, his silky fringe of a tail straight up in the air.

Matthew turned to her. "Look, I appreciate you coming in to introduce yourself but I'm afraid the job I have to offer wouldn't keep you interested. To be frank, I've hired overqualified candidates before and they left after only a few weeks. The job just isn't that interesting." He reached to take her hand and squeezed her fingers, giving her a smile that nearly made her knees knock together. She looked up into his caramel brown gaze and almost forgot to argue. It was refreshing to be able to look up into a man's face for once. Especially a face as yummy as Matthew Smart's. But with her hopes of gaining a job slipping from her fingers, Alex forced her mind away from his thick, dark blond hair, square jaw and kissable lips.

She held onto his hand when he would have pulled

away. "I'll go. But I wanted to make sure you knew that man just lied to you."

He narrowed his gaze. "Lied? What do you mean?"

She moved closer, lowering her voice. "You saw how he tugged his ear and looked at his shoes before telling you his daughter was murdered? Classic signs that someone is about to tell a lie."

"You think he's lying about his daughter being murdered?"

"No. Well, not necessarily. I just think Mr. Snow may know more about her death than he's letting on. Judging by the bruises on his knuckles and face he's recently been in a fight. It might be nothing, but I wonder. He also has perfectly manicured nails and an expensive haircut, telling me he has money. Yet his clothes are worn and thin. There's a tan line where a watch used to be. It makes me wonder why he removed it. His slacks are a quarter inch shorter than they should be and the buttons on his shirt are strained as if the shirt is too small for him. He looks like he dressed himself in someone else's clothes."

Matthew stared at her for a long moment and Alex felt panic swirling in her chest. She'd gone too far. He thought she was crazy. She expelled a sigh and gave him a smile. "I'll go now. I just…" Shaking her head, Alex turned toward the door. She had her hand on the knob, the door open, before he spoke.

"Alex. Don't go. You're hired."

# CHAPTER THREE

Their new client was standing in front of Matthew's bookshelves when he and Alex entered the room. Max stood in front of the door, his tiny body vibrating and a soft growl rumbling in his throat. His tail drooped to clearly show his displeasure with the man standing across the room.

Snow turned to Matthew as he came through the door, his dark gaze sliding to Alex and then quickly away. It was more than clear from his body language that he didn't approve of Alex. Matthew had to wonder why. Just to see how he'd react, Matthew did the formal introduction he hadn't done when Snow first entered the Smart Investigations offices. "Mr. Snow, I'd like to introduce my assistant, Ms. McFadden."

Alex shook hands with Matthew's new client. "It's nice to meet you, Mr. Snow."

Snow eyed Alex up and down, his lips thinning with obvious displeasure. "I guess it's casual Wednesday here at Smart Investigations, Inc.?"

Matthew gave the man a half smile. "Please, sit. Tell us why you're here."

Snow lowered himself to the client chair in front of

Matthew's desk and Alex took a chair a few feet away, her intense gaze fixed on Snow. As soon as she sat down, Max stopped growling and trotted over to her, jumping onto her lap.

"As I said before, I want you to find out who killed my daughter."

"How was your daughter killed?"

"Hit and run. She was out jogging yesterday morning and a car hit her, knocking her into a ditch and then speeding away."

Matthew frowned. "I'm sorry, sir. That's horrible."

Snow nodded, scowling at the floor. Matthew decided much of the hostility Max and even Alex were reacting to was probably just anger and grief. Anyone who'd lost a loved one in the way Snow described would be understandably angry. "Were there any witnesses to the crime?"

Matthew pulled a notebook close and jotted down Snow's initial statement.

"Yes. An old woman was coming out of a quick shop nearby. She told the police a big, black car hit my daughter and drove away."

"Do you have the woman's name?"

Snow tugged his ear, pursing his lips. "The police wouldn't give it to me. I don't think she's going to be very helpful anyway. It was very early and still mostly dark. The woman's eyesight apparently isn't very good. The police told me she couldn't give them much information."

Matthew scribbled on his pad and looked up. "Do the police have any reason to think this was deliberate?"

Snow glared at Matthew, his lips tightening. "They don't think anything. That's why I'm here. Someone killed my baby girl and I want you to find him. After all, I think you owe that much to her."

Matthew blinked. "I'm sorry? Why do I owe your daughter something?"

Snow looked astounded. "You don't know?"

Matthew slid Alex a look and she met it with a blank expression. He had no idea what she was thinking. "I'm sorry, Mr. Snow. Know what?"

"Roberta had an appointment with you yesterday. She was applying for the position Ms. McFadden apparently just took."

Ah. And that was why Mr. Snow didn't like Alex on sight. "I'm so sorry. No. I hadn't put the pieces together." Matthew tapped his keyboard to bring up his schedule. And there it was. Tuesday at four pm, Roberta Snow. A sense of deep sadness filled him. He couldn't remember what he'd been thinking when the young woman didn't show for her appointment. He was sure they hadn't been charitable thoughts. Guilt swirled uncomfortably in his belly. Matthew dropped back in his chair, the air escaping from his lungs in a sigh.

Snow stood up, handing Matthew a pile of cash and a business card. "Your website said you needed a thousand dollar retainer."

Matthew frowned at the cash. It was an odd way to be paid a thousand dollars. "Yes. My rate is $120 an hour plus expenses."

Snow nodded. "My private cell number is on this card. Call me as soon as you know anything." After a last scathing look toward Alex, he left the office.

~SC~

They sat without speaking for a few minutes. Alex watched her new boss type notes from the meeting into his computer. She was glad for the time to observe him in his element. Given the fact that he was about six foot five of yumminess, she decided she'd be happy to observe him any time. Her gaze slipped over the thick, dark blond hair, the square jaw, wide mouth, and short beard that made him look sexy and slightly dangerous.

When Matthew finally looked her way, his caramel brown gaze was intense. "Okay, what were your impressions?"

She dug her fingers into Max's silky fur and frowned. "Anger. Lots of it. Directed, I think more at me than the driver of the hit and run."

Matthew nodded, his mouth tightening. "Well, at least now we know why." He shook his head, his hand dropping down to cover the pile of resumes neatly stacked beside his keyboard.

Alex had made a note of the printed documents when she shook the client's hand, along with the dish of chocolate mint candy she fully intended to ravage later. She'd wondered where her own resume was in the pile.

Matthew reached beneath his desk and pulled out a small, black trashcan, foraging around inside it. "I threw her resume away yesterday, thinking she was just a no-show." Two lines formed between his dark blond brows. "I feel bad about the things I was probably thinking when she didn't show for the interview."

Alex leaned forward, placing Max on the ground. "You couldn't have known. Don't beat yourself up about it." She stood, preferring to move as she thought. Pacing was her chosen vehicle for pondering. "Aside from being majorly pissed at me, Mr. Snow seemed very certain about the facts of the case the police would let him have. It's unusual for a grieving loved one to be so forceful. I almost wonder if he has a law enforcement background."

Matthew's brows rose. "I hadn't thought of that. Good observation." His fingers danced across the keyboard. "Anything else?"

"Yes." Alex hesitated, reluctant to say what she was thinking. He watched her carefully, the sexy caramel gaze narrowing as she continued to pace without clarifying. Finally, she stopped in front of him, tenting her fingers on the surface of his desk. "Guilt."

Matthew sat back, chewing the end of a pencil that looked like Max had already had a go at it. Apparently chewing pencils was Matthew Smart's chosen vehicle for pondering. "You think he killed his own daughter?"

She blinked. "What? Oh. No. Of course not. I just think if we dug into their background we'd learn that Mr. Snow wasn't always the best father." She shook her head. "I'm guessing he was married to the job or traveled a lot. Something like that. Now that she's dead he's set himself on a mission to avenge her death. Which would explain the forceful behavior and his anger at me because of his perception that I replaced his daughter."

Matthew chewed the pencil another few beats, staring at her. His gaze was unreadable. Finally he nodded, dropping the pencil on the desk and adding her observations to his notes. "Good job, Alex." He smiled up at her. "I think you're going to be a real asset to this office."

She felt inordinately pleased. Despite her pleasure, however, Alex shut down the smile that wanted to escape and simply nodded in acknowledgement. "Thanks. Now tell me about Cameron."

Matthew's mouth opened, his face clearly showing surprise. "Excuse me?"

A thin ribbon of panic swirled in her belly and Alex worried she'd pushed too hard. But in for a penny in for a pound. If they were going to work together he was going to have to accept how her mind worked. Because she was damned if she was going to hide her light for another insecure man. She pointed to the manila file on his desk. The word Cameron was written across the front in bold, black letters and beneath it the words, Why killed? "I assume that's an ongoing investigation? I'd like to help with it if you'll let me."

His long fingers slipped across the surface of the file and he frowned. She'd noted the stiffening of his shoulders when she'd said the name, and the way his gaze swam away. Guilt?

"If you don't want to talk about it…"

He shook his head. "Cameron was your predecessor."

He finally looked up into her eyes. "I hadn't decided if I was going to tell you about that."

Icy fingers of worry danced across her lungs, making it hard to breathe. "Why?"

He twisted his lips thoughtfully, finally picking up the folder and handing it to her. "He was murdered in this very office just ten days ago, Alex. I don't know why and I don't know who. I wouldn't blame you if you didn't want to work here." He stood up. "In fact, it was stupid of me to offer you the job without telling you." He offered her his hand. "It's been an honor meeting you. I'll send you a check for the day and I really appreciated your help on the Snow case."

The icy feeling in her chest deepened, wrapping her lungs in a painful grip. "You're firing me?"

"No. I…"

She took a step forward, clenching her fists. Down by her sneakers a plaintive whine reminded her that her new, four-footed friend might misconstrue the anger she was about to exhibit. So she did something she rarely did. Alex took a deep breath and forced herself to calm. She held Matthew's gaze. "Am I to get a vote on whether I want to stay?"

He started to shake his head and stopped. "Alex, hiring you was a rash decision. I realize now that I'd worry for your safety."

She frowned, getting angrier despite her better intentions. "Because I'm a woman?"

Matthew sighed. "I know it sounds bad."

Alex reached behind her back and yanked out a tiny derringer, focusing it on the kill zone at the center of Matthew's chest before he had time to blink.

Max yelped in alarm, climbing her pant leg.

Alex lowered her arm, quickly slipping the gun back into the waistband of her sweats. "I have a concealed carry license. I spend time at the range every week and in the summer I regularly drive down to take advantage of the advanced courses at Camp Atterbury. I'm deadly at fifteen feet, dangerous at thirty, and pretty darn scary at forty." She leaned forward, resting her hands on the edge of his desk. "I can take care of myself, Matthew. And I want this job. Now how do we get to a meeting of the minds on this?"

She held her breath as Matthew stared back at her, his gaze darkening with emotion. Alex knew she'd gone too far pulling the gun on him. She was pretty sure she'd blown it. But given the chance she'd probably do it again. She'd be a partner to Mr. Matthew Smart or she'd be nothing at all.

Matthew crossed muscular arms over his chest and his face darkened. She was just about ready to thank him for his time and leave when he nodded. "I'm willing to give you the job on a trial basis. But only if you promise you'll never, ever draw on me again."

He didn't smile but his lips twitched slightly. If she hadn't been focused on his expression, Alex might have missed it. As it was, she had to frown to cover her pleasure. Shrugging, she headed toward the door. "It's a deal. As long as you don't piss me off." She turned and finally let the smile break free.

He looked shocked for a beat and then laughed, shaking his head. "I'm going to have my hands full with you, aren't I Alex McFadden?"

She pulled his office door open. "Yes, Matthew Smart. I believe you are."

# CHAPTER FOUR

Alex chewed her salad as she studied the neatly typed report on her desk. Behind her, she heard Matthew talking to Max as if he were a little human and it made her smile. She speared a cucumber and lifted it to her lips, her gaze sliding over the report. She was looking for something…anything that would lead to information about why Cameron had been killed. Shunting the page aside, Alex stared at the picture of personal affects the police had taken from her predecessor's pockets. There was a keychain with a bent ring and three keys. One key she guessed opened his apartment door. One matched her own key to the Smart Investigations office, and the third key looked like it might go to a padlock or a lockbox. She'd have to ask Matthew about that. Alongside the keys was a bent and battered thesaurus and next to that was a crumpled mint candy wrapper.

"Are you done with lunch?" Matthew came out of his office, Max bounding along behind him. The doxie jumped up on the chair she'd put alongside her desk and lifted his paws up to the surface to peer into the cardboard box. He wagged his silky tail with excitement, a slight under bite catching one side of his lip in a crooked smile.

The box chirped happily and, sensing the dog's presence over their makeshift nest, two baby birds opened their beaks wide and fluttered tiny, useless wings.

Matthew peered into the box too. "Tell me again where you found these two?"

She shook her head. "Just outside the office. Their mother was flying back to the nest and didn't quite manage to avoid the grill of the trash truck." Alex pinched a piece of cricket between her fingertips and dropped some of it into each tiny beak.

Matthew grimaced. "Please tell me you didn't chew that first?"

Alex grinned. "Not for long."

Matthew shuddered. "You want to come along with me to talk to the police about the Snow case?"

She didn't hesitate. "You bet." Grabbing her purse, Alex closed the Cameron file and stood. She caught Matthew staring at the file, a thoughtful look on his face. She decided it was as good a time as any for her to ask him some questions about the case. They headed for the door, Max bouncing past them with his whole body vibrating in excitement. "I noticed that whatever had been on the end of Cameron's keychain was missing. Do you know what it was?"

Matthew opened the door for her. "A flash drive. He carried information on cases between home and work on it. That way he could work from home if I needed him to." Matthew frowned. "He was a hard worker."

Alex shoved aside a surge of jealousy. She couldn't shake the feeling she was filling big shoes when it came to the recently departed Cameron. "Did the police take his laptop into custody?"

Matthew pointed down the street. "The car's down here."

Alex nodded, falling easily into step beside him. Matthew Smart had long, quick strides but Alex was tall too and had habitually put a few miles of running in whenever possible in a long-term, unending battle with about twenty extra pounds. She had no trouble keeping up with him.

"His laptop was gone."

"Stolen by the killer?"

"It appeared that way, yes. The desktop in his apartment was gone too and the place had been tossed."

"So the killer was looking for something. Any idea what?"

Matthew sighed. "I wish I did. Cam was just a regular guy. He walked to work every day. Worked right through lunch, and most nights he went to the gym after work." Matthew shrugged. "He worked a lot of nights from home. He was a bit of a loner, more interested in learning about investigations than socializing."

She smiled. "He wanted to become an investigator?"

"He did. And with his work ethic he would have been a damn fine one." Matthew sighed. "He was a good guy. I miss him."

Alex didn't say anything because it wasn't her place. She hadn't known Cameron and she'd benefitted from his death. As tawdry as that was, she couldn't regret that she'd found Smart Investigations. "Is it possible he'd been working on something of his own? Something that got him killed?"

Nodding, Matthew held the passenger side door of his MKX open for her and waited while she slipped inside. "It's the only thing that makes sense. None of the cases he and I were working on were dangerous." Matthew started the car and pulled smoothly away from the curb. "If Cam was working on something it would have been on that flash drive. We need to find it."

She liked the sound of that "we". "The small key on his keychain…I'm guessing that was to a locker at his gym?"

"Yeah. I searched it thoroughly and there was nothing in there but stinky socks, a squashed piece of chocolate, a couple of sweatbands and a basketball." Matthew shook his head. "To tell you the truth, I'm glad you're looking at the case. I'm stumped."

Alex nodded. "You searched his place?"

"I did." He turned to her. "Would you like to look too? If Detective Hanks is done with the place, we can stop by after we talk to her."

"I'd love that."

Traffic was light and they made it to the precinct in a little under twenty minutes. Matthew held the door for her and waited while she preceded him into the low-profile brick building. Alex thanked him, secretly pleased at being treated like a woman again. Rather than just a sex object.

"Hey Matt! What brings you down here today?"

Matthew stiffened as he turned to the burly cop behind the public desk. "Peaches, how are you?"

The big cop chuckled, shaking his head. "You need therapy on that name thing, man."

Alex glanced at Matthew and he gave his head a single shake. She figured that meant he'd explain later. "I'm here to see Detective Hanks. She's expecting me."

Peaches nodded. "I'll let her know you're here."

As the big cop picked up the phone to call Detective Hanks, Alex lifted a questioning eyebrow at Matthew.

Her new boss grimaced. "His name is Peachtree. He's always giving me a hard time about my name, so a while back I started giving him a hard time right back."

~SC~

"CSU found no DNA evidence except your assistant's," Cindy Hanks told Matthew.

"So the killer either wore gloves or wiped the scene down."

She shook her head. "He didn't wipe the chair down. It contained Cam's DNA."

Matthew frowned. "Okay. What about the rope, or the ceiling fixture it was tied to?"

"Skin debris on the rope. All Cam's. Not surprisingly

within reach of the noose, given defensive grasping. In fact Cam's fingertips were torn, bloodied from scraping on the rope."

Stars burst before Matthew's gaze and his stomach roiled. Her words painted an ugly and terrifying picture of his assistant's last moments. "Okay." He narrowed his gaze. "I feel a 'but' coming."

Cindy Hanks skimmed Alex a glance and sat on the edge of her desk, the heels of her hands resting on either side of her. "I'm afraid we found Cam's DNA farther up the rope too. And his fingerprints on the fixture the rope was tied to."

Matthew held her gaze, willing her to deny what she was implying. Or laugh and tell him she'd gotten him… Tasteless as a joke would be in that moment, it was far preferable to what Matthew knew in his gut she was telling him. "Cam didn't commit suicide, Cindy."

She shrugged, her gaze sliding away. "There were no scuff marks on the floor in front of the chair, which you'd suspect from a man who was being strangled against his will."

Matthew shook his head. "Even if Cam had been trying to commit suicide, which I'm denying to my last breath, once he started to die it would have taken a monumental will not to fight to live. He would have kicked out desperately, just as he apparently tried to pull the rope away from his throat."

"So what's your explanation?"

Matthew frowned.

"His shoes were off," Alex offered.

Matthew and Cindy turned to her. Silence beat against his new assistant for a beat but she didn't back down from her assertion. Instead she added, "Have them check his feet. If the killer pulled his shoes off before he killed him and then put them back on post-mortem, it's possible he broke a small toe or something. At the very least there might be post mortem bruising."

Detective Hanks frowned. "Are you serious?"

Matthew's chest burned with excitement. He gave Alex a smile. "If the killer tried to jam Cam's shoes on right after death it could still have caused bruising, yes." He turned to Cindy. "Call the ME. See if there's any bruising."

She sighed, walking around behind her desk and picking up her phone. A beat later she was talking to the medical examiner's assistant.

Matthew gave Alex a thumb's up. "Good thinking."

She shrugged. "It might be totally off the wall."

"That's the kind of thinking that solves cases. Any criminal worth his salt will try to fool the cops and muddy up the investigation."

Cindy disconnected. "No broken toes. No bruising."

Alex nodded, clearly disappointed.

"But…"

His head shot up. "What is it?"

"It might be nothing but the toe nail on his left big toe was torn."

Alex straightened. "Bleeding?"

"Not much," Cindy said. "It's probably nothing, Matthew. He could have torn it fighting the rope at the end. It doesn't prove it wasn't suicide."

Matthew nodded. "Not conclusively, no. But it's a start." He stood up. "Any sign of drugs in Cam's system?"

"Nothing in the blood or tissue. Urine on slacks was clean." She frowned. "But if the killer used something like GHB…"

"Gamma-hydroxybutyrate," Matthew interpreted for Alex. "A date rape drug that works very quickly and is hard to detect."

Alex nodded. "Stomach contents?"

Cindy perused what Matthew assumed was the ME's report on her monitor. "Coffee. High levels of magnesium and calcium…"

Matthew frowned, "Supplements?"

"Did he have stomach problems?" Alex asked.

"Yes," Matthew admitted. "Of course. He ate antacids like candy."

Cindy shook her head. "No wonder he had stomach issues if all he ingested was coffee."

"Cam generally only ate dinner. He always told me he wasn't wired for early noshing." The memory brought with it a sudden wave of sadness. "I actually ended up increasing his salary because he never broke for lunch."

Alex's pretty eyes filled with pity, warning Matthew he was letting his emotions climb too close to the surface. He shook it off and pushed his thoughts in another direction. "I picked up a new client yesterday."

Cindy leaned forward, placing her chin in her hands. "Oh?"

"The father of a hit and run victim. He insists his daughter was murdered."

Cindy turned to her computer. "Victim's name?"

"Roberta Snow. Age twenty-five. I had her resume on my desk."

Cindy's head shot up. "Really? That's eerie." She tapped a few keys and bent closer to the computer, reading quickly. "Yes. Hit and run. One witness."

"An older woman coming out of a quick shop?"

"Yes." She frowned. "How'd you know that?"

"The father told me."

She shook her head, sighing. "One of the uniforms must have blabbed."

"He's convinced it wasn't an accident. Did the cops find anything at the scene to imply it wasn't?"

"Signs of skid marks leading up to the hit. A slight hesitation as if the driver were panicking…thinking…then the squealing of tires as the car fled the scene. It's classic hit and run."

"Can we talk to the witness?"

She hesitated only a moment. "Sure. I'll send her information to your cell."

"I'd also like the key to Cam's place. Alex would like to

go over and take a look."

Detective Hanks nodded. "I'll have Peachtree get it from Evidence for you."

"Thanks." Matthew started toward the door. "You'll call me if you find anything in Cam's background check?"

Cindy nodded. "Of course. But my money's on something more current. If he was murdered…"

Matthew held the door for Alex and she slipped through, leaving the warm sent of vanilla sugar in her wake. "There's no if on this, Cindy. Cam was murdered. And we're going to find out by whom."

He closed the door on Cindy Hank's doubt-filled glance. Alex waited for him in the hallway, her expression carefully neutral. "What's next?"

Matthew moved past, clenching his fingers against the desire to touch her arm. If she'd been a man he could clap her on the back. If she were a man he could squeeze her shoulder in a moment of thankful comradery. If she were a man he could smack her on the ass…

He really wanted to smack her on the ass.

Shaking off the totally inappropriate, career ending thought, Matthew pointed down the hall. "First we rescue Max from Peaches. Then we go visit Ms. Snow's mother. Hopefully we can at least make some headway on one of our cases today."

Nodding, Alex fell into step beside Matthew as he navigated the confusing hallway system leading from the Interview rooms to the front desk. "Why did we have to leave Max up front with Officer Peachtree? I thought you two were inseparable."

Matthew sighed. "Mostly we are, but Max has been banned from the offices and interview rooms."

Grinning, she asked, "Banned? Why?"

"He doesn't like them—there must be bad juju in there or something. He always pees on the table legs."

Alex laughed, the husky sound sliding over his senses like warm butter. "Max is allergic to lies?"

"Something like that." Matthew grabbed the door a uniformed cop had opened, nodding a silent thanks. The cop gave Alex the once over, his gaze flaring with interest. Matthew glared after the man, briefly considering reporting him for overt sexual harassment. Then he shook off the thought, recognizing it as borderline cray cray. After all, if every man with inappropriate thoughts about a beautiful woman got into trouble…they'd all constantly be in trouble.

Alex nodded. "I'm with him on that. Perpetual liars are uncivilized and dangerous people."

"Not to mention they make our jobs harder by a multiplier of ten."

She grinned, turning as a happy yip greeted them from the front desk area. "There is that."

# CHAPTER FIVE

Cam lived a few blocks from the Smart Investigations, Inc. office. His small, studio apartment was in an old warehouse building that had been subdivided into a dozen or so living spaces. Though the lobby, elevator and stairs were all created in the retro style—heavy on metal, rivets and well-aged wood—everything was tidy and clean and the air smelled fruity rather than musty as Matthew always expected.

Alex was unnaturally quiet as they climbed the wide staircase to Cam's second floor apartment. He glanced her way, noting that she seemed awestruck, slipping her fingers lovingly over the carefully crafted details of everything they passed. "I take it you like retro?" Matthew asked her with a smile.

She made a small sound that could have been a moan. "This is like my perfect place." As Matthew inserted the key, she sighed. "But I'm sure it's way too rich for my blood."

He shoved the door open and allowed her to enter before him. "Don't be too sure about that. Cam managed it just fine. And since you're within walking distance of the office and almost everything else you need, you wouldn't need a car." He didn't mention that he'd seen her rusted blue bump of a car and figured she'd be relieved to sell it.

Or park it in a sink hole and walk away without looking back.

Alex chewed her bottom lip, a tic Matthew was beginning to recognize as her attempt to keep pleasure or excitement at bay. The thought made Matthew sad. Alex McFadden must have suffered a lot of disappointment in her life for her to instinctively resist pleasure that way.

The place looked just about the same as it had when Matthew had been there before. Cam's few belongings were thrown about the place, the floor was littered with what looked like pieces of mail, which had probably been sitting on Cam's desk when the apartment was ransacked. Pillows and cushions were ripped, their stuffing littering the floor, and paintings were thrown into the middle of the one- room apartment, their surfaces brutally sliced. Dishes and glassware lay shattered among the debris.

"This looks as much like rage as anything else," Alex said with a frown. "Whatever Cameron did, he really hacked somebody off."

Matthew nodded. He'd gotten the same impression when he'd searched before. "I looked through everything," he told Alex. "Even searched the floors for loose boards where he might have stashed something."

Alex's eye caught on something across the room and she started toward it. Matthew realized she was heading for the old register beneath the windows. "I looked that over pretty good."

Alex crouched next to the register and ran her fingers along its bones, finding nothing. She stood and looked around again. Her gaze slid skyward. "Did you search that chandelier?"

The pitted steel and crystal chandelier centered in the room was made to look old, but Matthew knew from getting up close and personal with it that it was new. "Yup. And let me tell you examining each of those crystal teardrops was not fun."

She grinned. Her gaze slipped past him and widened.

Matthew turned. "What is it?"

She knelt before a large, ornate vent cover and placed her hand in front of it. Warm air wafted from the metal duct Matthew could see behind the grate, gently swirling the heavy silk of Alex's mahogany hair. "I take it the register is just for show?"

Matthew walked over and crouched down beside her. Her warm, vanilla sugar scent cold-cocked his senses and something low in his body tightened and hardened at her nearness.

"Are you okay?"

He blinked, realizing she was looking at him with a worried expression.

"I'm fine." His gaze slipped over the full softness of her bottom lip and he couldn't help wondering if she would taste as good as she smelled. Matthew turned away before he grabbed her and pulled her in for a kiss...or a tumble on the littered floor. In desperation, he fixed his gaze on the grate before them. The twelve inch square grate covered a metal duct that provided the room's heat. On an impulse, he tucked his fingers into its retro swirls and tugged it off the wall, setting it aside. He did a visual scan of the back of the grate and then peered into the duct, running his fingers around inside just to make sure it was empty. "Nothing."

She nodded, standing.

Replacing the cover, Matthew pushed to his feet. "Whatever Cam had he either didn't keep it here or the killer already found it."

"Right." Alex sighed. "Oh well, it was worth a try."

Matthew followed her out of the apartment, his gaze determinedly focused away from her perfect, round behind. She was wearing a short sweater set in a soft ivory color that looked amazing with her dark hair and chocolate brown slacks that hugged her curves like a lover's caress.

Matthew's jeans tightened at the inappropriate thought and he nearly groaned. She stopped short and he ran into her, every nerve ending in his body exploding with pleasure at the unexpected touch. The groan he was trying to squelch escaped before he could stop it and he found himself looking into her exotic gray-blue gaze.

Time stopped and Matthew forgot to breathe.

Alex didn't move away. She didn't look away. Instead, she licked her lips and Matthew's body turned to steel as wave after wave of sheer, sizzling need assailed him.

She bit her lip. "You sure you're okay? You seem…"

He pulled breath into his lungs and suddenly found himself within a few inches of her delectable lips. So close, in fact, that the soft peaks of her breasts pressed against him, sending a fresh wave of lust razoring through him. "I'm fine. It's just…hard…" He swallowed, at a loss for an explanation that wouldn't send her shrieking for the nearest exit.

Her eyes widened in alarm.

Too late, he realized what he'd said. "Being here, I mean. At Cam's place," he clarified quickly. "It's difficult to be here again."

The alarm in her gaze turned to understanding and then, dammit, pity. Matthew didn't want her pity. He wanted her naked and writhing beneath him. "We should get out of here."

"Yes." But she didn't move, didn't slide her exquisite gaze from his, and Matthew had to clench his fists to keep from grabbing her. Finally, just when he thought he was going to lose the battle, she turned away. "Shall we go interview Mrs. Snow?"

"Yes," he said with too much relief in his voice. "That's the logical next step." Uh, uh, his body argued. It wasn't. The logical next step was for him to kiss Alex senseless and then remove her clothing piece by piece until he could taste every inch of her body…

No! Matthew told himself. That's not logical at all.

It wasn't logic that was riding him hard. In fact, it was about the furthest thing from logic. But dammit if he didn't want to throw reason aside and grab pleasure with both hands.

Just once.

~SC~

Alex and Matthew sat on a hard, contemporary style couch in an immaculate and unwelcoming living room, Max nestled between their feet on the floor. The little dog stared across the space at the woman sitting in an equally hard looking chair across from them. Her red nose and puffy eyes bore witness to the fact that she'd been crying, but her hair and makeup were in place and she was dressed as if she were going somewhere nice.

Leanne Snow was probably in her mid-fifties but looked forty. She had a thick mane of blonde hair that showed no signs of graying. Her elegant face was unlined, her frame slim and athletic. She lived as if she had money but didn't act like she was rich.

Alex liked the woman and had no trouble putting herself in Leanne's place, feeling the other woman's pain at the center of her chest, like a slow, painful burn. "I'm so sorry for your loss, Mrs. Snow."

The woman sniffed, dabbed the end of her red nose with a clean tissue and nodded. "Thank you, Ms. McFadden." She lifted the business card Matthew had handed her. "I'm surprised to hear that John hired you to investigate Roberta's death." She shook her head, her lips tightening just enough to show anger. "He never showed much interest in her when she was alive. He hasn't even called me since..." The words drained away, her pretty face going slack with grief. She rubbed her arms and looked past them, shaking her head.

Matthew leaned forward, placing his forearms on his knees and clasping his hands. His handsome face was filled with compassion, his voice gentle. "Your husband wasn't around much?"

Leanne shook her head, her gaze sliding to a framed photo of her daughter on a table nearby. "John was in the military. He's been in Hawaii at the base there since January. I didn't even know he'd returned."

Alex and Matthew shared a glance. "Was it unusual for your husband to return to Indianapolis without contacting you?" Alex asked.

Mrs. Snow reached toward the photo, stretching a long finger toward the shiny silver frame as if to touch it. But she didn't touch the photo. Instead she clenched her fingers and looked at Alex. "We've been divorced for two years, Ms. McFadden. It wasn't a friendly divorce." She shook her head. "No. It wasn't unusual. In fact I would have been surprised if he had contacted me." Tears filled her eyes again. "But it would have been nice if he'd told Roberta he was in town. She still loved her father. Even though she rarely saw him."

"Mrs. Snow. Do you have any idea why anybody would want to kill your daughter?" Matthew asked.

The woman blinked, horror transforming her pretty features. "Kill Roberta? You mean murder? You think my baby girl was murdered?"

Alex reached over and clasped the grieving mother's hand. "Your husband seemed to think she was. The evidence points to an accident. We're just trying to make sure that's all it was."

The woman relaxed slightly. She shook her head. "Nobody would want to kill Roberta. She was the sweetest thing. Pretty and soft spoken. Everybody loved her."

"Was it normal for her to go out running every morning?"

Mrs. Snow nodded. "She's...she had always been a runner. She said it was her time to think...to plan."

"Did she always take the same route?"

The older woman's gaze sharpened on Matthew. "You still think someone killed her."

Matthew shook his head. "I have to ask, Mrs. Snow."

Alex squeezed her hand. "Mr. Snow hired us to find out." It wasn't strictly true, but it seemed to soothe the other woman a bit.

"Why would your ex-husband think someone murdered Roberta," Matthew asked.

Leanne's brown eyes sharpened. "John's just feeling guilty because he knows he should have protected her. He should have been there for her when she needed him, but he's never been here for either of us."

"Did your daughter need him, Mrs. Snow?" Alex asked. "Was Roberta having some kind of trouble in her life?"

The woman's gaze turned guarded. "Trouble? Nothing that should have gotten her killed." She tugged at the wet tissue in her hands, tears sliding down her pale cheeks. "She'd been tense lately. A little worried maybe…" Shaking her head again, she took a deep breath. "I guess it doesn't make sense to protect her secret now." She looked up, focusing a determined look at Matthew. "Roberta was pregnant. She'd decided to keep the baby."

Alex's heart twisted with new pain. "Oh God, Mrs. Snow, I'm so sorry."

Sensing Alex's sadness, Max rose up on his back paws and placed his forepaws on her thigh. She dropped a hand onto his soft head and he happily wriggled his butt.

The other woman nodded. "Thank you. It's why she moved back home. So I could help. And she was trying to find a job so she could buy the things she'd need. For the baby…"

A soft sound of exquisite pain wrenched free from Leanne Snow before she could stop it. She lifted a shaking hand to her lips as if to block the agony from escaping. "I told her she didn't need to work. I have money. I could have taken care of both of them. I would gladly have done it…"

"Can you give us the name of the father, Mrs. Snow?"

Leanne Snow grimaced. "She told me he's married."

She shook her head. "He wanted nothing to do with Roberta or a baby."

"Do you have his name?"

The woman shook her head. "I'm sorry. She wouldn't tell me. But I think he worked at the campus."

"IUPUI?" Alex asked.

"Yes. From what Roberta told me he was older. Probably one of her professors." She put a fist over her mouth, swallowing a sob. "He really hurt my little girl, ya know?" Her watery gaze found Alex's, no doubt assuming another woman would understand.

Alex did understand. All too well. She gave Mrs. Snow's hand another squeeze. "I'm so sorry."

Mrs. Snow gave up trying to hold back the sobs and crumpled under her pain.

Max bounced over to the weeping woman and jumped up in her lap before Matthew could stop him. "Max! I'm so sorry, Mrs. Snow."

The woman shook her head and pulled Max close, burying her face in his fur as she gave in to her grief.

~SC~

He watched them leave the Snow house and smiled. They were doing exactly as he wanted them to do. So predictable. So ineffective. He almost wished they'd give him a bit more of a challenge. It wasn't going to be any fun if they were playing Checkers while he was playing a world class game of Chess.

They stopped beside Smart's navy blue SUV and stood talking, their body language telling him they were on the edge of a bond…each straining toward something they both knew they shouldn't explore. But from the way Smart reached out to touch her, his gaze locked hungrily on her pretty face, it was clear he was losing the battle against his feelings. And he didn't see the woman trying to put any distance between them either.

The thought made him frown. She was much too good

for Smart. Intrigued by the woman, he'd checked up on Miss Alexis McFadden. What he'd discovered had been impressive. Genius level IQ. Multiple advanced degrees. And a singular ability to underachieve with all her smarts.

All that stood between her and spectacular success was her own insecurities. He would have liked to add Alexis McFadden to his collection. But unless she proved herself worthy…

They climbed into the car and Smart pulled out into the street. The woman's gaze slipped over him as they sped past, not even seeing him in his baggy clothes and stooped posture. He smiled beneath a rangy mustache and quickly straightened, dropping the hedge trimmers he'd grabbed from an unlocked garage and heading for his car. He needed to determine if Leanne Snow had told them anything she shouldn't have. And if she did…well…she'd be joining her daughter in Hell.

~SC~

Matthew hung up from his call with Detective Hanks and took Alex's elbow as they climbed a steep set of concrete stairs. "Cindy's going to find out who Roberta Snow's professors were and figure out if one of them was the baby's father."

Alex grimaced. "Do you really think he'd kill her over a baby? It's not like society expects much from baby daddies these days."

Matthew shook his head. "It seems unlikely. But people have killed for less. Especially if they're trying to protect a marriage."

"True."

Matthew jerked his head toward the door at the top of the stairs. "This is it."

Pansy Blithe lived in a senior residence on the North end of town, only a few miles from where the Snows lived. The quick shop she'd been leaving when Roberta Snow was killed was only a mile away from the attractive building that housed her apartment. On the way over, they'd decided to examine the accident scene after talking to the witness, so they could view it with all the information the police had.

The residence units all had exterior entrances, with large numbers beside each forest green painted door, so Pansy's apartment was easy to find. "There it is," Alex pointed to a door at the end of the first building. "Number One Hundred and Ten."

The woman who answered the door when they knocked barely scanned them a look before her gaze slid down to where Max was sniffing her Welcome mat. She clapped age spotted hands together and squealed, causing Max to jerk his head up and tuck his tail. "You brought Rodney!"

To everyone's surprise, Pansy Blithe bent down and scooped Max up and then turned and walked back into her apartment, the hesitant swing of a shaggy tail showing under one elbow.

Matthew lifted an eyebrow and Alex grinned. "After you," he said with a sweep of his hand. He closed the door behind them and looked around, finding the small, clean space filled almost to bursting with an eclectic mix of furniture, some of which belonged in a high end antiques store.

They followed the sound of cooing and found Mrs. Blithe offering Max, who stood happily atop the kitchen counter, a piece of sugar cookie. Max snarfed up the treat and, his tail wagging manically, kissed the old woman on her nose.

"You certainly know the way to a dachshund's heart," Matthew told her.

She laughed. "Rodney's always loved my sugar cookies." She turned a delighted smile toward them. "He loves Fig cookies too but they give him gas." She giggled, lifting Max off the counter and squeezing him tightly enough to elicit a muffled yip of alarm.

Alex hurried forward. "Why don't you let me hold him, Mrs. Blithe. I see you were in the middle of making tea."

The woman frowned as Alex scooped Max out of her arms but nodded. "You're right dear, I was making tea. Would you like some?"

Matthew started to shake his head.

Alex gave the woman a mischievous smile. "Only if it comes with a couple of those cookies. They look delicious."

"Of course, dear. Have a seat." She busied herself gathering mugs and spoons and settling them on the table with a plate of cookies. Max strained toward the plate and, when Matthew wouldn't let him eat a cookie, stretched his neck as far as he could and swept the air with his tongue.

"Here, Rodney, dear…" Mrs. Blithe settled a plate with a cookie onto the floor.

Alex put him down and he hurried over to munch the sweet, his fringe of a tail whipping happily.

"Milk?"

Alex nodded, a cookie poised before her luscious lips. "Yes, please." Matthew found himself watching carefully as she took a bite, fighting the desire to scoop a residual sparkle of pink sugar from her mouth as she chewed.

"Young man, you look hungry."

Matthew turned to find Pansy Blythe grinning conspiratorially at him, her wet, hazel eyes sparking with amusement. His face heated under the sure knowledge that he'd been caught ogling his new assistant. Quickly grabbing a cookie, he reconsidered his initial assessment of Mrs. Blythe. She was much sharper than he'd assumed.

She poured tea from a pretty ceramic pot and then sat down, watching Max lick the empty plate hopefully. "What's his name?"

Matthew blinked. He'd assumed by her initial reaction to seeing Max that she'd mistaken him for a dog she once had. "Max."

She nodded, her gnarled hands settling over her round

belly. "He's a handsome boy. My Rodney looked just like him." She frowned. "Except maybe a bit more tan over his eyes."

Matthew sipped his tea, finding it delicious.

Alex finished her cookie and reached for another one, grinning at Matthew when she saw him noticing. "My salad left me a couple of hours ago. My blood sugar is crashing."

Matthew felt instantly guilty. He hadn't even asked if she needed anything. He was used to working with Cam who never ate during the day. "I apologize. I'll remember next time to ask about your blood sugar."

She nodded, chewing happily. "Actually, that's a lie. I'm just a sucker for sweets so I tell myself I'm hungry when I'm not."

Their hostess laughed. "I used to do that too, dear. When I was young enough to care about how I looked. Now I just eat what I want when I want it. Life is beautiful."

Looking into the old woman's happy face, Matthew didn't doubt it. "I'm sorry to bother you, Mrs. Blythe…"

She waved a hand at him. "Please. Call me Pansy. And you're not bothering me at all. I love having visitors."

He smiled. "Good. We're investigating the hit and run death of Roberta Snow and we wondered if you could tell us exactly what you saw that morning?"

Pansy's eyes grew wide. "That poor little girl." She pursed her lips. "That man didn't even slow down. If I hadn't seen it with my own eyes I'd have never believed it." Shaking her head, she broke a small piece of cookie off the one on her plate and tucked it between her lips, frowning.

"You saw the driver?" Alex asked.

"Oh yes, dear. He was in his fifties, though he had that ugly thing old men do…you know…where they're bald in the front so they grow their hair out too long in the back?" She grimaced. "Men should just learn to accept what nature does to them as they age."

"I agree," Alex said, twisting her lips to hide a grin.

"Can you start at the beginning, ma'am? What was the first thing you saw when you came through the door?"

"Actually I saw headlights skimming across the front of the store just before I came outside. I think the car had turned from Maple Street. I heard it accelerating as I came outside. It was really loud, like the muffler was bad or something."

"You know cars, Pansy?" Alex asked with a grin.

"You bet your sweet butt I do, dear. My papa used to let me help him work on our cars when I was little."

"Okay, so the car that hit Roberta Snow was loud. You say it was accelerating toward her?"

"That's what it sounded like. I was fussing with my bag at that point, thinking I'd forgotten to get the half 'n' half." She placed a soft hand over Matthew's on the table, patting him. "I'm getting very forgetful in my old age, son. It's a trial." She thought about her problem for a moment and then went on. "When I looked up there was a big, dark colored car or minivan veering directly toward that little girl. It happened so fast I'm not sure about the make of the vehicle. I think it was a van. But I recognized the girl because she ran past my house every morning at about the same time. She was a pretty young thing." Pansy shook her head, clearly disgusted. "That car headed right for her. I thought he was going to go into the ditch but the headlights swept over the girl and then she turned, her pretty face looking all shocked, and she tried to step out of the way." Pansy leaned forward, her expression angry. "That man turned the wheel into her. He didn't slow, didn't hesitate, he ran into her and then, when she flew off the side of the road he stopped and I heard a window go down. It was like he was looking to see if she was moving."

"He didn't throw on his brakes in an attempt to avoid hitting her?" Alex asked. "The police said there were skid marks."

Pansy shook her head. "No. He didn't hesitate. He headed right for her."

Matthew wasn't sure how much of what she was telling them they could believe. It was highly possible John Snow colored her recollections of the event. "Pansy, have you spoken to Mr. Snow?"

Her hard gaze softened. "Her father? Yes. He stopped by yesterday. Poor man. He's a wreck."

Matthew skimmed Alex a look and her eyes widened, telling him she'd noticed. John Snow had lied to them about talking to Pansy. "Did he tell you that he thought his daughter was murdered?"

Pansy broke off another bite of cookie and chewed it thoughtfully. "He just wanted to know what happened."

Her response was just unspecific enough to cause Matthew's spidey senses to fire. "He asked you if you thought the car hit his daughter on purpose?"

Pansy sipped her tea. "I'm not sure. I don't remember." She stared off into space for a moment and then glanced down at the floor. "Would you like some tea, Rodney?"

# CHAPTER SIX

Matthew crouched down and examined the skid mark leading to the shoulder. "These marks look narrow for a van tire."

"Maybe Pansy was mistaken about the make of the car," Alex told him.

He grinned. "Is it possible our star witness could have been mistaken?"

"Well I don't know, Rodney."

He chuckled. Straightening up, Matthew walked over to the spot on the gravel shoulder where, judging by the direction of the marks Roberta Snow would have been thrown. He examined the long grass in the ditch, looking for a flattened area. He didn't find one.

Alex crouched down and touched something in the gravel. "Glass. Looks like a headlight."

Matthew frowned. "I don't remember a broken headlight in the accident photos."

She picked up a sliver and handed it to him. "It's definitely headlight glass."

Matthew pulled an evidence bag from his shirt pocket and slipped the shard into it. "I'll have the police compare it to the glass they must have found right after the accident. Apparently I missed that in the photos."

She shook her head. "I didn't notice a broken headlight either."

Matthew's frown deepened. "From the officer's report Roberta should have landed right here."

Alex walked in the direction he pointed, examining the spot like he had. "That's strange."

Matthew walked down the road a few feet and pointed to a flattened spot in the ditch. "That looks like the spot we're looking for. But if the car hit her there…"

"She couldn't have landed in that spot," Alex finished for him. Alex descended into the ditch and walked carefully around the spot. After a moment she reached down and rubbed a finger carefully over a place where the grass had been gouged away. "Come look at this."

Matthew crouched next to her. "Is that an earring?"

Using her phone, Alex took a picture of the earing in the dirt and then picked it up between two fingernails, holding it up so Matthew could see it. It was a tiny cross dangling from a gold hoop. "What do you want to bet this belonged to Roberta Snow?"

"You from the police?"

They looked up to find a man walking across the road toward them. "About the accident?"

Matthew stood and turned, extending his hand. "Matthew Smart. I'm investigating the hit and run."

The furrows in the man's brow cleared. "Oh. That young girl." He nodded. "That was terrible. I thought maybe you were here about the other one."

Alex came up beside Matthew. "I'm Alex McFadden, Matthew's assistant. How are you?"

The man clasped her hand, his narrow face flushing as she looked him in the eye. "Pete Bogs. Nice ta meet ya. I manage the Quick Stop across the road there."

Matthew frowned. "There was another accident in this spot, Mr. Bogs?"

He nodded, dragging his gaze away from Alex and

fixing it on Matthew. "It was a busy day." He shook his head. "One of those tiny cars was sideswiped by a guy on a motorcycle. He was weaving in and out of cars and cut it a little close. The driver of the car threw on the brakes to keep from hitting him." Bogs pointed to the spot where they'd found the glass. "But not before the guy's tire took out a headlight." He shook his head. "I reported the guy for reckless driving but the cops didn't ticket him. They blamed the woman in the Smart Car for failing to yield." He shook his head. "I was hoping you were from the police and were going to do something about this stretch. People drive too fast through here."

"So these skid marks are from the earlier accident?"

The man nodded. "I believe so. Why?"

Alex and Matthew shared a look. "The police report ruled the girl's death an accident based on these marks," Matthew told him.

The man scrubbed a hand over his jaw. "That's odd."

"Yeah. It is," Matthew agreed. "But since we have you here, is there anything you can tell us about the hit and run accident, Mr. Bogs?"

"No. Sorry. I was in the back room when it happened."

"Can you hear road noise back there?" Alex asked him.

"Usually I can. In fact it was warm that day so I had the window open."

"Did you hear a horn or squealing tires?"

"No. All I heard was a thump. I knew something or someone got hit. I wasn't kidding about this stretch of road. People drive too fast through here so there are a lot of accidents. I hear that sound a lot I'm afraid."

"When you heard the thump did you run outside to see what had happened?" Matthew asked.

"Yeah. I asked Pansy what happened and she told me a jogger had been hit. That the car sped away." He shook his head. "How can somebody do that?"

"You didn't see the car?"

"No. But Pansy said it was big and dark. Had one of

those oval shaped yellow stickers on the back window."

Matthew's eyebrows lifted. "She told you that?"

"Yeah. She's pretty sharp." He caught Matthew's startled look. "She's a regular at the Quick Stop."

"Do you know what the sticker said?" Alex asked.

"I do. I've rented cars from them myself a few times. It's stupid to pay top dollar for a rental car, in my opinion."

Matthew nodded. "What rental company, Mr. Bogs?"

"Bashin' Jack's. He has good cars. They just have a lot of miles on them and sometimes dents and stuff. He gives you a great deal on a three day rental. Me and Mrs. Bogs rented a Suburban there once for a long camping weekend." He smiled. "Those Suburbans hold a lot of stuff, let me tell you."

~SC~

"Bashin' Jack's?" Alex asked Matthew when they climbed back into his MKX. Max leapt into Alex's lap and proceeded to kiss her face while she giggled. She gently pulled him down and he curled into her lap, sighing happily.

Matthew nodded, glancing at his watch. "I think we have time. Can you send Cindy a picture of that earring and ask her if it's Roberta's?"

"Sure."

As he pulled away from the Quick Stop, Matthew's phone rang. He glanced at the ID and frowned. "I need to take this."

Alex nodded, turning to look out the window as they headed back into the city. She forced her attention away from Matthew's private conversation and stared out the window, her mind working the facts as she knew them. The stretch of road they were on was a bit desolate. Not a lot of homes or businesses lined either side of the narrow, winding road and visibility was bad with all the hills and trees. Not a good road for a young woman to jog on. If someone wanted Roberta Snow dead, the accident on Mars Road across from Pete Bogs' Quick Stop was the perfect spot for it. Mr. Bogs had said it himself. The road was a common spot for accidents. In fact, the killer had gotten lucky with the skid marks. That mistake by the cops had put them totally off his scent.

"Alex?"

The undertone of impatience in Matthew's voice told her she'd been buried in her thoughts. He'd probably been talking to her for a few minutes. She shook her head. "Sorry. I was just going over some things in my mind."

He nodded. "We'll have to go to the rental place in the morning. There's something I need to take care of."

She nodded. "Anything I can help with?"

He started to shake his head and stopped. "Actually, maybe there is. That was Cam's sister. She's at the office. I haven't really spoken to her since his death."

Something tired and frustrated flared in Alex's breast. Despite her high IQ and extensive education, men still seemed to think her best attribute was her ability to relate on an emotional level rather than an intellectual one. She nodded, responding with just a tinge of pique in her tone. "And you'd like a woman there in case she's weepy."

To her surprise, Matthew frowned. "Well, no. I actually was hoping to make use of your powers of observation. If Stella's holding anything back about her brother's activities, I'd like you there to suss it out."

Alex's eyes went wide. She immediately felt guilty for assuming Matthew was like all the other men she'd worked for in the past. "Oh. Sure. I can do that."

An uncomfortable silence descended between them. It was clear to Alex that she'd offended her new boss. She needed to try to make things right between them, but explaining her sensitivity would take a lot more time and get into a lot more detail than she was interested in covering at that early stage of their relationship. So she bit her lip and resisted the urge to babble an apology. She was determined to show Matthew Smart that she was a worthy partner. She'd earn his respect by being useful rather than by whining at him about past abuses. With that thought in mind, Alex turned to Matthew. "Tell me about Cam's relationship with his sister."

"Their relationship. Let's see. Well, they were close. Really close. They'd lost their parents a few years earlier so they were alone as far as immediate family. Stella's older and she's married with two kids. Since their parents died…"

"How'd they die?"

Matthew shook his head. "They were skiing in Nepal and got caught in an avalanche."

"Wow."

Matthew skimmed a look her way. "Yeah. Freak accident. Cam took it really hard. The only way the two of them got through it was by leaning pretty heavily on each other."

"So if Cam was into something that got him killed, Stella might know something about it."

"That's what I'm hoping. I don't see him keeping it from her. But he might not have given her any details. Cam kept his work pretty close. That's my fault, I'm afraid. I was always drilling it into him that our reputation depended on our being circumspect. We often hold people's deepest secrets in our hands and if we're careless with them, we won't last long."

When he slid a look in her direction, Alex realized his words were directed at her. She made a key turning motion in front of her lips. "I'm a vault."

The intensity in Matthew's handsome face slipped away as he smiled. "Nice to meet you Vault, I'm Safe."

She shared the smile. "Safe? Really? I wonder."

And just like that, the smile slipped away and something hot and sexy slid across his gaze.

# CHAPTER SEVEN

Stella Rodriguez was standing at Alex's desk when they came into the office. She turned as Matthew came through the door and smiled, her dark brown gaze warming when she saw him. But then she spotted Alex behind him and the heat left her gaze, turning decidedly chilly.

In Alex's arms, Max barked a happy greeting, his tail whipping against her hip.

Stella smiled. "Hi, Max." She enfolded Matthew in a hug that smelled of roses and sunshine. "How are you, Matthew?"

He held her tight for a moment, sharing his friend's loss with the only other person in the world who understood his pain. "I'm okay." He put her at arm's length and gave her the once over. The dark ovals of her eyes were underscored by purple circles and she was pale under the thick wave of dark brown hair. "You look tired."

Stella shrugged, stepping away. "I've been having trouble sleeping." She covered her mouth with a shaky hand. "I keep dreaming about Cam. He's asking me to help him." A single tear formed a silver trail down her cheek. She sniffled, swiping almost angrily at the moisture. "I told myself I wouldn't blubber like an idiot in front of you."

Matthew pulled her close again, kissing the top of her head. "You can blubber all you want. I can take it."

Stella shook her head and pulled out of his embrace, fixing a cool gaze on Alex. "Hello, I'm Stella Rodriguez."

Looking slightly uncomfortable, Alex took Stella's hand and shook it twice before dropping it like a hot potato. "Alex McFadden. It's a pleasure to meet you, Stella."

Matthew noted the way Alex avoided telling Stella her new role, realizing she'd feel funny about announcing that she'd replaced the brother Stella was grieving. "Alex has kindly offered to help me out for a while." He could almost feel his new assistant stiffening over his words, realizing as he said them they implied he was just going to use her to help him get things back under control and then send her packing. He hoped she understood he was just trying to soften the blow for Stella. "Let's go into my office and get comfortable."

Stella finally looked away from Alex. But rather than letting Matthew guide her into his office, she pointed to the cardboard box on Alex's desk. "Did you know there are two baby birds on Cam's desk?"

Alex made a small sound of alarm. "I need to feed them." She hurried around behind her desk and opened the drawer where she kept the mashed bugs.

Matthew clasped Stella's arm. "You don't want to watch this. Trust me."

Stella's gaze widened. "She's not going to chew the bugs and barf them up is she?"

Alex laughed, the sound a husky presence sliding over Matthew's nerve endings. "I mashed the bugs up pretty good so they can digest them." Stella moved closer and watched with apparent delight as the babies rose up, beaks open and squawked loudly to be fed. Alex pinched some mashed bugs between her fingertips and dropped a bit of the mess into first one tiny beak and then the other.

Stella's face transformed. "That's amazing."

"Alex is a rescuer," Matthew said with a grin. His gaze caught on Alex's and something undeniable passed between them. Something that Matthew realized would cause all kinds of trouble if they allowed themselves to explore it.

Alex pulled out a wet wipe and cleaned her fingers. "Would you like some coffee or tea, Stella?"

"No." She finally favored Alex with a smile. "But thank you."

"My pleasure."

"Shall we get comfortable," Matthew urged.

Stella allowed herself to be guided into his office. She took a seat at one of two client chairs facing his desk. As Alex took the other chair, she turned to her. "I always rescued things when we were growing up. Cam loved to make fun of me for it." Her gaze fluttered downward at the memory and Alex reached over, clasping her hand. Then she reached toward the glass dish of candy and plucked two mint flavored chocolates out of the dish. "I don't know about you, Stella, but my blood sugar's crashing." She handed one of the mints to Cam's sister. "I always said there was nothing much that chocolate couldn't make just a little bit better."

Stella took the mint, turning it over in her fingers as she frowned. "Cam hated chocolate."

"He and I had that in common," Matthew said. An awkward moment of silence followed, wherein Matthew struggled to find the words that would ease Stella's pain.

Alex took a second mint. "Well, I love it." When Stella looked up, Alex winked at her. "I'm thinking Matthew's candy allowance is going to be stretched while I'm here."

Stella's lips turned up in a sad smile and then she laughed. Finally she peeled the foil off her candy and took a tiny bite.

Matthew could have kissed Alex for creating that smile. "You said you needed to talk to me, Stella. Was it about Cam?"

She swallowed the chocolate, nodding. "I wondered if you'd made any progress on finding out who killed him."

He hesitated, unsure if the police had told her about their ridiculous suicide theory. "We've been working on it. I spoke with Detective Hanks this morning."

Stella made a face, pursing her lips. "That woman doesn't have a clue."

"I take it she told you about her new theory."

Turning to Alex, Stella nodded. "There's no way Cam committed suicide."

Despite her strong statement, Matthew couldn't help noticing the way her lips trembled. "Did he seem off to you in the days leading up to his death?" he asked Stella. "Had he mentioned any problems? Anybody who was bothering him?"

She shook her head. "No. If anything he seemed happier. He was really excited about his job and he loved working here." She slid a speculative gaze toward Alex. "He even told me he'd started working toward opening his own office someday."

"Did he elaborate on that?" Alex asked.

Stella shrugged. "He was taking classes at night in business and crime studies."

Matthew leaned forward, placing his elbows on his desk and looking directly into Stella's eyes. "What about his cases? I'd noticed lately that he was extra busy. Busier than his workload should have caused. Is it possible Cam was investigating his own case?"

Stella thought about the suggestion for a moment. "It's possible. He'd become fascinated by a case in his Crime and Criminology class. A serial killer. He was studying the guy's history and MO. But I don't think it went beyond academic interest."

"Do you remember the killer's name?"

"No. Cam marked the textbook up though. You should be able to find it in there."

Matthew shook his head. "There were no textbooks in

Cam's apartment or here."

Stella frowned. "That's strange. His computer maybe? If he was making notes or even writing a paper on the guy that would be on his laptop."

"The laptop was missing when I came in that morning. The killer probably took it."

Stella's eyes grew wide. "That's it then. It has to be tied to the case Cam was studying. Maybe he found something the killer didn't want anybody to find."

Matthew nodded. "I'd bet money on it. Cam was damn good." He reached across the desk and clasped Stella's hand. Her skin felt cold but she turned her hand and squeezed his back. "Find this jerk, Matthew. Not just for Cam, but for all the people he might kill if he's not stopped."

"If this is the guy who killed Cam I'll find him." He glanced at Alex. "We'll find him."

Pleasure blossomed on Alex's face. She nodded, her hand sliding stealthily over the small pile of candy wrappers in front of her.

Matthew almost smiled. He stood up and Stella stood too. "Thanks for coming to see me, Stella. It was nice to talk to someone who knew and loved Cam like I did."

Her eyes glistened with unshed tears as she nodded. Matthew walked her to the door. She hesitated in the doorway. "I wanted to tell you that Cam's funeral is on Thursday. I was hoping you'd say a few words."

"Of course." After Stella left, Matthew turned to Alex, noting the tiny piece of chocolate on her bottom lip. "It looks like we're heading back to school tomorrow."

She grinned, her tongue sliding unerringly over the speck of chocolate. "Sounds good." She grabbed her purse off her desk, along with box of birds. "I'll see you at eight?"

"See you then." Matthew started toward his office. He had a few emails to answer and some calls to make before he went home. Sensing Alex's hesitation, he turned back.

"Thanks for everything you did today, Alex. You were a great help."

She nodded, her eyes showing the pleasure she wouldn't allow her face to express. "Good. I'll see you in the morning then. Night, Matthew."

"Goodnight, Alex. Take care."

Dropping into his desk chair, Matthew checked his emails and spotted one from his sister. He grinned. Tandy was twenty years old and tended to view life through a forest of exclamation points. Every text or email from her was written in nearly ALL CAPS!!! The email he opened was no different and had the unhappy addition of several smiling puppy icons littering its contents.

HEY BIG BROTHER!! I know you're SICK of having people ask you how you are…and have subsequently bitten the heads off all your other siblings when ASKED!! So I won't…ask that is. I'm just going to say I LOVE YOU!!! and tell you that if you need help at the office I'm HERE!!! xoxoxoxoxoxo Love, Tandy.

Matthew's reply was a quick, I love you too. Thanks for checking in. Everything's good here. He hoped the note would put the kibosh on any idea of Tandy coming into the office to "help out". In that moment, Matthew was eminently grateful for Alex. If he had to spend every day listening to his younger sister babble on her cell phone to all her girlfriends about men, he just might lose what was left of his mind.

Matthew's phone rang and Max's head snapped up. It was Hanks. "Hey, Cindy. What's up?"

"I wanted to let you know the earring you found was Roberta Snow's."

"Okay. Thanks. Then the skid marks were not from her hit and run."

"It appears that way," Cindy agreed. "I also got a call from Leanne Snow. She said somebody broke into her home when she ran to the store and broke a lamp. She has no idea who it was or what they wanted. The back door was kicked in so it most likely wasn't a pro. I told her it was probably just kids. Just in case, I dispatched a cruiser to keep an eye on her place."

"That's strange."

"It is, but I don't think it's anything to worry about. I'm just covering all the bases."

"Thanks for letting me know."

"Of course. I'll talk to you soon."

Matthew disconnected and sat staring through the office door into the outer office. The news of a break-in at the Snow residence bothered him. He wasn't sure why. It was probably just the timing. He didn't believe in coincidences and the happenstance of someone breaking into the Snow residence was more than he could dismiss. He was glad to hear Cindy took immediate action. He could concentrate on the investigation of Cam's death and let the police deal with the other piece.

~SC~

He watched the woman leave the office and head toward her silly little car. Unseen behind the wheel of his rented truck, he took the moment to watch her walk, appreciating her fine, full-figured form. She was a beautiful woman. There was no doubt about that. But like the man before her, she had the potential to become a problem.

He watched her climb into her rust bucket of a car and pull away from the curb, then slid his gaze away, tugging the brim down on his ball cap as she passed by. Waiting a few beats to put space between them, he joined the flow of traffic following her down the street. Away from Smart Investigations, Inc.

It just might be time to reach out and touch Miss Alexis McFadden. It had been too long since he'd watched the life drain from another's eyes.

And he was feeling restless.

A monster clawed for release beneath his skin when he was restless. And the longer he tried to ignore the monster, the bigger and meaner it became. He'd discovered just how mean when he'd taken a few months off from letting the monster roam free.

Matthew Smart's assistant learned it the hard way. It hadn't been a pleasant way to die.

He smiled, thinking he might enjoy letting the monster out on beautiful Miss Alex. All too soon, she pulled her little car over to the curb and climbed out, locking it before looking both ways down the street, her hand shoved inside her purse. For just a brief moment, her gaze slipped over the truck, hesitating, and he noted the lines between her brows that told him she was leery.

He turned his face away as he passed her, driving on by as if he were looking for another address. And when he checked the rear-view mirror a few beats later she was gone.

Something warm and pleasurable bloomed in his gut. The monster purred with pleasure. She would be a worthy adversary. He would have to be on his guard with that one. The pleasure blossomed, bringing hot, expectant blood to the spot which throbbed in anticipation of their meeting.

He'd found his next playmate. And the monster more than approved his choice.

# CHAPTER EIGHT

Alex was sitting at her desk when Matthew came in the next day. He frowned when he saw her, immediately recognizing the strain tightening her shoulders. "You're here early."

Her head came up and she fixed that sexy gray-blue gaze on him. "Morning."

Matthew cut the distance between them and placed a tall cup of coffee and a small bag onto her desk. Her gaze widened as she eyed the bag. "Is that what I think it is?"

"If you're thinking it's a cheese Danish from Pandora's Bakery you'd be correct."

She grabbed up the little brown bag and opened it, holding it up to her nose and closing her eyes on a pleasure-filled groan. "You are the best boss in the entire world."

He chuckled. "You earned it yesterday." He started toward the door as she pulled the moist pastry from the bag. He knew exactly what she was about to experience because he'd already eaten his. But he wasn't prepared for the sensuality of her moan when she took her first bite. He turned to look at her and found her eyes closed, head tilted back as if she waited for a lover's kiss. A speck of pastry sat dead center on her full, kissable bottom lip. He almost groaned aloud when her tongue came out and swept the crumb away. "Good?"

Her eyes shot open and her cheeks pinkened. "No." She settled the pastry onto the bag and picked up her coffee. "I was just faking it."

He snorted out a surprised laugh.

Her eyes sparkled with mirth over the top of her coffee as she took a sip. "Delicious. Thanks for thinking of me, Matthew. That was very kind of you."

He shrugged. "I worked you pretty hard for your first couple of days." He let his lips curve upward in a slightly mean smile. "And you're probably going to work twice as hard today."

If he expected her to look chagrined by the news he was disappointed. To Matthew's delight, Alex nodded eagerly. "I can't wait to get started." She stood up and walked over to him, carrying a small notebook and mechanical pencil. "I thought we could have a quick meeting to kick off each day. You can tell me what needs to get done and we can discuss what we learned since the previous day."

Matthew felt his brows rise. "That's an excellent idea. Come on into my office. Don't forget your breakfast." He turned away before she could read the pleasure on his face. He didn't want her to get the wrong idea. Especially since it wouldn't exactly be the wrong idea. He was very attracted to Alex McFadden. So attracted, unfortunately that Matthew was doubting he would be able to keep her on. An office romance would be a huge mistake. Nothing good ever came from them. And that was assuming she even returned his interest. He'd seen very little indication that she did.

The realization depressed Matthew because he understood that, pushing aside his physical attraction to Alex, he would miss her presence in his life in a professional capacity. She was a natural investigator with stellar instincts that, in any other situation he'd love to shape and encourage.

"I hope you don't mind, I took the initiative to call Bashin' Jack's and make us an appointment for later this morning."

Matthew's head came up in surprise. "Oh. That's great. Thanks, Alex."

She sat down across his desk, settling her small pad onto the scratched wooden surface. "I figured you'd want to go by IUPUI later to talk to Cam's professor so I called over there and got his name and schedule. He has office hours from one to three."

Matthew blinked. "I'm impressed."

She shrugged. "I don't believe in waiting around to be told what to do. That isn't very helpful."

"Great. That will give us time to dig into Roberta Snow's life. She's got to have an enemy somewhere."

Alex smiled. "So you believe Pansy's story?"

"Not all of it, Rodney."

Alex giggled.

"But we now know that those skid marks belonged to the accident earlier in the day, so Pansy's observations were correct. It doesn't look like the driver tried to avoid hitting her."

"Do you know something I don't? I didn't think we'd definitely settled on the cause of the skid marks."

Matthew told Alex about Cindy's call the night before.

Alex nodded. "Should I contact Detective Hanks and ask for the report and photos from the morning accident?"

"No, I can do that."

"It's possible the driver was drunk or under the influence of drugs. Or maybe fell asleep behind the wheel. If that's the case it could have still been an accident."

Matthew nodded. "That would be another explanation. But we won't have that information until we find the guy."

"Right."

"I'd like you to find out what textbook Cam was using

in his criminology class. If Stella's right his investigation started there. We'll pick up a copy on campus when we go to meet with the professor."

Nodding, Alex made a note and then sat frowning, staring at her pad.

"What are you thinking?"

She looked up as if startled from her thoughts. "What? Oh, it might be nothing."

"Tell me."

"Well. It's just that, I'm guessing Cam wouldn't be pursuing an investigation unless he thought there were current cases."

Matthew's eyebrows lifted. "You're thinking he made a connection between something recent and something he read in his textbook?"

"It seems logical."

And Matthew should have considered it himself. "I'll ask Detective Hanks if she has any unsolved murder cases sitting around. Something where they don't have a strong suspect." He gave Alex a smile. "Good thinking." She stood and headed for the door, clearly uncomfortable with his praise. Matthew would have to help Alex learn to accept compliments. "What time are we supposed to be at Bashin' Jack's?"

"Ten thirty." She told him. "I map-quested the route. It will take about twenty minutes. Thirty if traffic's heavy."

"We'll leave at ten then. Thanks, Alex."

She finally gave him a smile. "It's my pleasure." She started to turn away and stopped, settling an intense gaze on him. "I do mean that, Matthew. I'm really enjoying my job here. I hope we can make it permanent."

Matthew sighed as she closed the door quietly behind her. How was he going to tell her he couldn't hire her on a permanent basis because he was too attracted to her? It was so totally unfair. She was more than qualified for the job. And she'd already proven her worth in a hundred different ways. He'd be the worst kind of monster to tell her she couldn't have the job.

Unfortunately, he didn't see any way around it.

~SC~

They pulled into the parking lot of Bashin' Jack's and Alex looked up from her notes. "The class uses three textbooks. But one of them is a book of true crime case studies. I'm guessing that will be our best bet."

Matthew nodded. "I agree." He pulled into a spot in front of the doublewide that constituted Bashin' Jack's office building and killed the engine, looking around. "Amazingly, I don't see a big black car with a dented front fender."

She gave a theatrical sigh. "Why must everything be so hard?"

He chuckled. "I guess if this job was easy anybody could do it."

She climbed out and looked around, her spidey senses tingling. Upon closer inspection, every car in the lot had some kind of dent in it, some clearly older, with rust painting the ridges, and some unidentifiable as far as age. Only two vehicles fit Pansy's loose description of large and dark, and one of those was a full sized van rather than a minivan. The other one was a navy blue pickup truck with a matching cap on the bed. They walked over to the van and examined the front, finding a lot of bugs but no dents. The pickup was old enough to have a metal bumper and it did have a dent in it, but it was on the wrong side of the vehicle to have plausibly been involved in Roberta Snow's hit and run and the dent was deep and narrow, like it had been rammed into a pole.

Matthew frowned. "I'll have Hanks send a crime scene tech over to test the dent for blood but I'm not hopeful. Neither one of these vehicles is the one we're looking for."

The door to the office slammed shut behind them and they turned to find an apple-shaped man with a shock of dark brown hair ambling toward them. "Mornin', folks.

You lookin' to rent a car?" The man lifted eyebrows that were like dense slashes over small, brown eyes and offered Mathew a beefy hand. He pumped Matthew's hand twice before offering the moist paw to Alex.

Matthew shook his head. "I don't see what we're looking for on the lot. Do you have a big car, black or dark blue with a dent on the front bumper?"

The salesman frowned. "That's pretty specific. Can I ask why you're looking for the car?"

Alex smiled. "We're not here to accuse you of anything, Mr. Bash. We're actually looking for the person who rented the car on Monday night or Tuesday morning early."

Jack Bash held her gaze for a long moment and then nodded. "Come with me." He led them around the doublewide to a gravel area that contained a large dumpster and several cars that didn't look drivable. Alex couldn't help wondering if Bashin' Jack's would try to rent the beaters to its customers. They slipped between a car with a punched in roof and a jeep with no tires. Bash stopped beside a large, mud-covered blue car, pointing to the front end. "I think you'll find what you're looking for on this Suburban."

Sure enough, there was a large dent on the front right quarter panel. Matthew crouched down and examined the dented area carefully and then scanned the grill. He pointed to a short, light-colored hair sticking out from the dented grill. "I'm guessing we'll be able to tie that to Roberta Snow."

Alex crouched down beside the grill, examining it carefully as Matthew pulled out his phone. "I'll call Hanks."

"This car hit somebody didn't it? Dammit."

Alex looked up. Jack Bash's eyebrows slashed downward, clearly showing his concern. "Why didn't you call the police, Mr. Bash?"

He shrugged. "I thought maybe he hit a deer or

something."

Matthew disconnected. "Mr. Bash, the police will be here shortly. I wonder if you'd answer a few questions for me before they get here?"

The man nodded. "Anything I can do to help. I don't want you people thinking I had anything to do with this."

"We'll need all the information you have on the person who rented this car."

Bash turned, motioning for them to follow. "It isn't much. I'm pretty sure the license and credit card he gave me were fake."

"Why do you think that, sir?" Alex asked.

Bash opened the office door and held it until Matthew grabbed it. "I tried to contact him after he dumped the car. The agreement he signed said he was supposed to fill the gas tank before returning the car. He didn't."

The office smelled like cigarette smoke. The walls were old, dark paneling and the floors were covered in cheap linoleum that curled up at the edges and crunched underfoot.

"He didn't leave any contact information?" Matthew asked.

"Of course. But the phone number didn't work and I did a lookup on the address. It's an abandoned building a few miles from here. I even drove by but nobody in their right mind would live there." He shook his head. "I was going to show the guy's photo around but the place was empty."

"Can we see the photo?"

Bash pulled a rusty metal drawer open in a file cabinet. He thumbed through some folders, squinting at their contents under the meager light coming through a single, cloudy window. A moment later he handed some pages that were stapled together to Matthew. The first page was the contract the man had signed. The signature was illegible, a sloppy scrawl across the bottom of the page. The second page was a picture of the lessee's license.

Matthew showed Alex the picture. She frowned. "With all that hair we'll never identify the guy."

Matthew sighed. His hair hung long and stringy to his chin and two furry rectangles that resembled caterpillars crouched over eyes that looked light blue behind oval shaped wire rims. The mustache under his veiny nose was full enough to curl down over his upper lip, obscuring its shape. A vee-shaped beard which was several shades lighter than the hair obscured his chin. "When did the man return the car?" Matthew asked Bash.

The owner of Bashin' Jack's shrugged. "He dumped it on the street about a mile from here. The lot's locked up after hours but customers park their returns in front of the gate if they need to. This guy didn't even bother to return the car. I'm guessing he didn't want the cameras to catch him returning it."

Matthew's brows rose. "You have cameras on the lot?"

It was Bash's turn to look surprised. "Of course. If I didn't my assets would disappear from the lot."

Alex chewed her lip as her gaze met Matthew's. She was pretty sure nobody would bother Bash's crappy inventory even if he left the cars running at night with balloons tied to their grills that said, "Come and get me."

"Can we see that feed?" Matthew asked the owner.

"Sure. Come on back to my office."

~SC~

Matthew stared at the man on the security tape as he limped toward the Suburban, his hands shoved into the pockets of his wrinkled khakis.

"That's a different guy," Jack Bash told them. "He's taller than the dude I rented the car to, and my guy didn't have a limp."

"So he paid somebody to rent the car and then he just drove it away," Matthew said. "Clever." Matthew pointed to the video. "He knows the camera's there. See how he averts his gaze?"

"He keeps pulling the bill of his ball cap down too. That's strange, since he's obviously wearing a disguise," Alex added.

Matthew nodded. "So all we've got is a man with, possibly light blue eyes who looks to be about six two, with a slight paunch and a limp."

"Most of which can be faked," Alex added.

"Yeah." Matthew scrubbed a hand over his jaw. "Maybe we'll get lucky and CSU will find prints in the Suburban."

A car door slammed outside and a moment later they heard a woman's voice in the outer office. "Speak of the devil," Alex said with a grin.

Matthew stood. "Let's go tell Hanks what we know and then get out of here. I think I want to stop by that building the killer listed as his residence."

She frowned. "You don't think he really lives there do you?"

"No. But people who are hiding sometimes exploit things tied to their lives. Even when they don't realize they're doing it. I just want to get a feel for the place. Maybe we'll get lucky and stumble upon a connection."

They stopped to talk to Hanks on the way out. She handed Matthew a piece of paper with three names on it.

"What's this?" he asked.

"The first name is the professor at IUPUI who was having an affair with Roberta Snow. Unfortunately he alibied out. He was in Chicago for an anniversary weekend with his wife at the time Roberta was killed."

"Dang. Okay. Who are the other two names?"

She peaked an eyebrow. "You don't recognize them?"

Matthew read the names again. "No. Should I?"

"Like Roberta Snow, both of those people had appointments with you for Cam's job."

Alex and Matthew shared a surprised glance. The first

threads of worry slithered through Matthew's gut.

Hanks pointed to the first name. Katrina Watts. "Mrs. Watts was run off the road by a man in a light-colored minivan on her way to her appointment with you. She filed a report a few days ago and when your name came up they brought it to me."

Matthew scrubbed a hand over his jaw. "I remember now. She did call and tell me she'd had an accident. And this guy?"

"Thomas Zepnick said he was grabbed around the throat on the street about a block from your office, pulled into an alley and threatened. A guy he never saw told him if he kept his appointment with you he would die."

"Good god!" Matthew exclaimed. Alex had gone pale. He reached out and squeezed her shoulder. "What the hell's going on, Cindy?"

She shook her head. "I have no idea. But, Matthew, the only way this guy could have known these two people had appointments with you was if he'd hacked into your computer or broken into your office."

"Cam's computer," Alex said.

They both looked at her. "We believe the killer took Cam's laptop, right? If he's at all computer savvy it wouldn't be hard for him to use it to find his way into Matthew's mail."

Matthew felt sick. "I guess that explains why I had so many no shows."

Cindy nodded. "I'm surprised Alex snuck through without being accosted." She fixed Alex with a speculative look.

"I didn't have an appointment," Alex told the cop. "I just stopped by on an impulse…" If it was possible, her face lost even more color. "Holy crap. If I hadn't made an impetuous decision to stop in that day…"

"I would never have gotten the best assistant I've ever had," Matthew finished for her.

She blinked in surprise at his statement. Matthew didn't

blame her. Even he was surprised he'd said it. But what was even more surprising was the realization that it was absolutely true.

# CHAPTER NINE

The abandoned building the Suburban lessee claimed as his address was little more than crumbling brick with twisted, fractured bones and a collapsed roof. The property was surrounded by a chain link fence with a wide open gate. The chain that had been holding the gate closed lay on the ground and the heavy duty padlock was next to it, the shackle cut clean through.

Matthew eyed the building and then skimmed Alex a look. "Maybe you should wait here."

She lifted an eyebrow and pushed through the gate ahead of him.

Matthew decided it wasn't worth arguing with her, but he didn't like it. There was a chance, small though it was, that they were about to confront a killer in the ramshackle building. When faced with a choice, his instinct would be to protect Alex rather than subdue a killer.

Matthew scanned a look over the front façade of the red, brick structure. The building slumped between two large old homes that looked to have been turned into multi-renter residences. He figured the tumbling edifice before them, sporting long narrow windows with broken glass and filthy curtains fluttering in the breeze, had once been a rental property too. But it was no longer safe. And the owner apparently lacked the will or the funds to bring it back.

As they got closer, Matthew noted the charred edges of the broken windows on the upper level and the jagged holes in the roof that had no doubt been created by firemen fighting the blaze. The old stench of smoke still clung to the building, clearly telling the story of its demise.

As he scanned the windows, he saw movement behind the one on the lower level at the far end. "Somebody's in there."

Alex nodded. "I saw her." She stopped at the scorched doorway and leaned in, listening. Nothing disturbed the silence except the soft cough of air sifting through the broken windows. She looked at Matthew and he nodded, quickly moving in front of her and sliding through the door first. The room beyond the door was tattered, its walls water stained and wires hanging down in dusty ribbons through holes ripped into the plaster.

Debris crunched under their shoes as they moved more deeply into the house, ultimately finding themselves in a surprisingly undamaged kitchen area. As soon as they stepped through the archway leading to the kitchen something swayed in the shadows of one corner and a form slipped out from under a table and brushed past them, running for the door. The man smelled of sweat and other unpleasant things and he shoved Alex to the side with filthy hands.

Matthew rushed forward to block the gaping back door. The man barreled into him, nearly taking him to the floor, but Matthew wrapped his arms around the vagrant, holding him in place.

Beneath the filthy clothing he wore, the man's frame felt skeletal.

"I don't want to hurt you," Matthew assured the struggling man.

"Let me go!"

Foul breath wafted over Matthew's face and it was all he could do not to cringe away. "I just want to ask you a couple of questions. It will only take a minute."

The man tried to stomp on Matthew's toes, his body vibrating with fear. Below a torn knit cap, hazel eyes over scored by shaggy brows darted wildly around the room. "I'll scream," the man warned.

Suddenly, a twenty dollar bill appeared before the struggling man's face. He stilled immediately, turning to look at Alex. She smiled kindly. "It's yours. All we want is for you to look at a picture and tell us if you've seen the man around."

The man's face folded into a frown but he finally nodded.

Matthew loosened his hold. "I'm going to let you go now. You'll get the money in just a minute."

Alex pulled the bill back and stepped away to give the terrified man some space. "Will you look at a picture now?"

The man nodded. Matthew handed the vagrant a copy of the picture Bash had given them. "This man may walk with a limp. He wears a dark blue baseball cap with no logo. Have you ever seen him around here?"

The vagrant took the sheet of paper between filth-blackened fingers. He stared at the picture for a long moment.

"Can you tell us who that is?" Alex urged.

"It's Gregg," a rusty voice said from the doorway.

Matthew and Alex turned to find a diminutive form layered in an oversized coat and fingerless gloves. A hunter's cap with flaps covered her head, making her small face look childlike beneath it. She was marginally cleaner than the man, but her eyes burned with fever and her skin was unnaturally pale.

"You're sick."

The woman shrank away as Alex approached, backing toward the door. "I'm fine." But she coughed harshly and it shook her frail frame.

Alex skimmed Matthew a look. "I have a friend who's a doctor. I can ask him to visit and check you out."

The woman shook her head, her eyes wide. "No doctors." She looked at the man. "We answered your questions. Now give him the money and go."

"One more question," Matthew said. "This Gregg, does he live here?"

"No," the man finally spoke. "He stays here sometimes but he moves around a lot."

Matthew lifted the sheet of paper the man had returned to him. "And he looks like this?"

"Not the beard and mustache," the woman offered. "Not anymore. He grows the hair when it's cold."

Matthew looked at Alex and he figured she was thinking the same thing he was. That Gregg, whoever he was, was hiding from somebody. "Is Gregg here now?"

The man shook his head. "A few days ago."

"Where does he stay when he's here," Alex asked.

The woman frowned, coughing against the back of her hand. "Upstairs. It ain't safe up there. But nobody bothers him." She shrugged.

Matthew nodded at Alex and she handed the money to the vagrant. He handed another twenty to the woman. "Thank you for your help. Are you sure you don't want help? You're clearly sick."

She shook her head. "I got no use for doctors."

He handed her a business card. "If you see Gregg again, will you contact me?" He reached into his pocket and pulled out a hand full of change. "There's a phone booth on the corner." She frowned, looking at the card, but after a moment she nodded.

Alex followed him to the steps. He stopped at the bottom, scanning a look at the rickety stairwell. "You should stay down here, Alex. These steps look dangerously unstable and I'm guessing the floor above is the same."

She frowned. "Then you shouldn't go up either."

"There's something you might not know about me. Before I became a private investigator I was a fire investigator. I know my way around a compromised scene."

She blinked. "Oh. Okay." She pulled out her cell phone. "I'm just going to make a call then."

Matthew nodded. "I'll take pictures of anything I find so you can see it."

Her smile made something heat and twist in his gut, shocking him with its power. Unsure how to deal with her effect on him, Matthew turned away and hurried up the stairs, nearly forgetting to watch where he was stepping.

~SC~

Alex stared at her cell for a moment before forcing herself to tap out a number from her past that she should no longer remember. She frowned as the phone began to ring. After the fourth ring she started to disconnect, but a deep, breathless voice stopped her. "Dr. Phillips."

Hearing his voice again, Alex nearly panicked and hung up on him. A beat later he tried again. "Hello?"

She forced herself to speak. "Ben. It's me."

His hesitation beat against her eardrums and made her pulse speed. Finally, he spoke. "Alex."

To her vast surprise, his voice was filled with warmth. Even a touch of longing. "How are you?" she asked the specter from her past.

"I'm fine. What about you? Are you still in Indy?"

She nodded and then realized what she was doing and did a mental head slap. He'd always had an ability to discombobulate her. It was one of the reasons she'd let their relationship go so far before stopping it. Doctor Ben Phillips was a drug Alex had trouble resisting. Unfortunately he felt the same way…about every woman he met. "I am. I'm working as a private investigator…" She glanced guiltily over her shoulder to make sure Matthew hadn't heard her silly lie. But her pride wouldn't allow her to tell him the truth…that she'd sifted through job after job since leaving medical school. Ben would believe her discontent was tied to him. To their breakup.

"Seriously? Well, I guess that makes sense. You were always the best student I knew with the diagnostic portion of medicine. Congratulations."

Alex heard the question in his voice. He was wondering if she was calling because she wanted to get back together with him. The realization spurred her on. "That's why I'm calling, actually. I'm looking for a suspect and ran across this homeless woman…"

Alex could almost hear him straighten up with interest. "Okay." Did she hear movement in his voice? Despite his loyalty issues, Dr. Ben Phillips was the most compassionate physician she'd ever known. Regardless of the potential risk to his career, he'd never stepped away from an opportunity to help someone who couldn't help herself. "What are her symptoms?"

"Weak, pale, clammy. She has a really bad cough and her emaciated state is probably exacerbating things."

"Right. Okay. Give me her location."

Just like that. No hesitation. No awkward questions about why she'd called him after two long years apart. It had been one of the things that she'd loved about him. No. Love wasn't nearly strong enough. Alex had worshiped the man. And when she'd learned about his betrayal, it had been the impetus for her leaving the program. Medicine no longer held any allure for Alex.

She gave him the address. "She's here with a man. He might be her husband. I don't know. But they're very leery of strangers."

"No worries. I'm dressed in my usual getup." She heard self-deprecating humor throbbing in his deep voice and couldn't help smiling.

"Oh good. They'll think you're homeless too."

When he chuckled good naturedly, Alex suddenly found it hard to breathe.

"Will you be there?" he asked.

"No." Realizing she'd nearly shouted her response, Alex quickly clarified. "I'm leaving now. Thanks, Ben."

"Anytime, beautiful. You know that, right?"

She filled her lungs with air. "I've got to go."

"Alex?"

Her eyes dropped closed. "Yes?"

"It's been amazing to talk to you again. I've missed you."

"Goodbye, Ben." She hung up before she gave in to the need to tell him she'd missed him too. It would give him encouragement where he shouldn't feel any. More importantly, it was no longer true. It had been for a while but not anymore. Or was it?

"Alex?"

She jerked around, shoving the cell into her purse in a movement that felt guilty. "Hey. Did you find anything useful?"

Matthew eyed her for a moment, his sexy gaze seeming to pierce clean through her. Right to the core of her confusion. "Yeah." He held a laminated rectangular document out, grasping it on the edges so he wouldn't smear any existing prints. Alex took it the same way, scanning the familiar face on its surface. "It's him."

"Yeah. I also found these." Matthew held up a small baggie that contained some long brown strands that looked like hair. "They're synthetic but they could definitely be from the wig he probably wore."

She grinned. "We've got him."

Matthew didn't seem to share her enthusiasm. "Yeah, but we still don't know who he is. And the fact that he left these behind tells me he doesn't plan to return."

She nodded. "He's probably too careful for that." She handed the license back to Matthew and he slipped it into a second baggie.

"We'll give this stuff to Hanks. Maybe we'll get lucky and the crime lab will find a print on the license."

Alex preceded Matthew out of the building and walked alongside him in silence as they headed back to his car. He waited until they'd climbed into the MKX and pulled out into traffic before asking. "Are you all right? You seem…I don't know…distracted is the right word I guess."

"I'm fine." She bit her bottom lip, wondering if she should tell him about Ben. Finally, she settled on just telling him what she'd asked her former lover to do, avoiding the topic of their relationship altogether. Her love life really wasn't any of Matthew's business. Yeah, she frowned, she'd keep telling herself that. But deep down she knew that her fascination with Matthew would make it his business if they ever acted on the attraction they clearly shared.

She did a mental head shake. They would never act on it. Because she'd done that once and it had been the worst mistake of her life. It had cost her not only her happiness, but it had also cost her a career she'd thought she loved. And in the process it had made her cynical where men were concerned.

Alex would never make that mistake again.

# CHAPTER TEN

Professor Reginald Deets was in his office when they arrived. Matthew knocked twice and a voice called out for them to enter. He pushed the door open and motioned for Alex to precede him. The man behind the desk had long, blond hair that showed gray at the temples. He wore it pulled back in a thin ponytail. His narrow face was tanned and sported a tidy patch of hair on his chin and a thin mustache. His eyes were brown, his mouth wide. Deets took one look at Alex and surged to his feet, unfolding his tall form from behind his desk with an outstretched hand. "Hello, my dear. Are you here for the assistant's job?"

He had a slight accent that Matthew thought might be British, but he couldn't rule out Australian either. The accent was too faint; obviously he'd been in the States a long time.

Matthew stepped forward, offering Deets his hand. "I'm afraid she's with me." Out of the corner of his eye, Matthew saw Alex glance his way. She seemed surprised.

"And you are?"

"My name is Matthew Smart. This is Alex McFadden. We're investigating the death of my assistant, Cameron Rodriguez."

"It's nice to meet you, Professor Deets." Alex's voice held a note of censure and Matthew studiously avoided her gaze.

Deets frowned. "Ah, yes. Cameron was a good student. He was very diligent." Tugging the cuffs of his sweater down over his wrists, Deets nodded toward a couch across the large, cluttered office. He waited for them to sit down and then lowered his gangly form into an upholstered chair near the couch. "I was devastated to hear about Cameron's death. He was in my history of theatre class too. I'd grown very fond of him." Sadness transformed his smug features and Matthew realized the professor probably wasn't lying about his relationship with Cam. The genuine emotion made him seem a little less arrogant. "Can you tell me what happened to him, Mr. Smart? The police were very vague."

"Just that he appears to have been murdered. Alex and I are trying to find out who and why."

Deets nodded. "Of course. I'll help you in any way I can."

"We believe Cam might have been following up on something he saw in one of his textbooks, Professor Deets," Alex said. "Can you give us any idea what that might have been?"

"Actually, I probably can. Cameron had been an adequate student, turning in all of his homework in time and attending nearly all of his classes. But his work lacked a certain…" Deets brushed at the knee of his charcoal gray slacks. "I guess the word is, heart. Until we started the serial killer segment. Cam seemed to come alive over those case studies."

"Was there a specific case study that he was interested in?" Alex asked.

"I couldn't tell you. I know he was writing about one of them for his final paper. If you can find that you'll have your answer."

"Unfortunately Cam's laptop was stolen the night he was killed."

Deets' eyebrows peaked. "You don't say? That's astounding. So there was something on his computer that might implicate his killer. Fascinating."

"That's what we believe, yes," Matthew agreed.

Alex leaned forward, her expression pleasantly intense. "Professor Deets…"

"Please, call me Reginald." His smile was warm to the point of embarrassing.

Alex blinked under its force. But she regained her composure so quickly Matthew doubted that Deets even noticed. "Of course. Reginald. Did Cam come to you looking for additional information? Maybe requesting other resources for his study?"

"Yes, he did. How very smart of you to ask."

Matthew bit back a smile as Alex barely caught herself from rolling her eyes. In that moment he thought he understood her wish for independence and respect a little more. He doubted Deets was the first one to underestimate his beautiful assistant. "Alex is extremely intelligent, Professor. And highly educated. I'm lucky to have her."

Alex's gaze slid to his and held, full of speculation. With a start he realized she assumed he was ridiculing her accomplishments. "But she's very humble," he quickly added.

Shaking her head, Alex seemed to be fighting a smile. She turned her attention back to Deets, obviously waiting for his response to her question.

"Cameron did come to me a week or so ago. He told me he was writing his paper on one of the killers from the case studies and I told him I was happy to hear it. I asked him if he wanted suggestions for additional reading and he deferred. Instead he asked me a series of general questions about the type of killer."

"What questions, Professor. Can you remember?"

He turned to Matthew. "He wondered if a serial killer could change his method of killing."

Alex cocked her head. "And you told him it was highly unlikely."

Deets nodded. "Yes. As you no doubt know, this type of killer suffers from what we refer to clinically as antisocial personality disorder. More generally referred to as psychopathy. They have no conscience…no sense of right or wrong…and therefore see people simply as objects to be manipulated to their own ends. Many will fixate on a certain event in their lives when designing their kill plans. Of course the killing is merely the final act of the psychopath's carefully crafted plan. The build up to the kill is arguably the most important part. That pathway, if you will, to the ultimate act of killing is formed through years of planning and crafting to create the final scene that depicts a specific outcome. Any change in that pathway interrupts the fiction the killer is trying to create."

Matthew thought about that for a moment. "But presume the buildup to the kill remains the same. Would it be possible for the killer to change the method of killing and keep the fiction intact?"

Deets shook his head. "As I told Cameron, it's highly unlikely."

"Unless the killer isn't a true psychopath," Alex offered.

Deets' eyes grew wide. "Why Alex, that's very astute. A few paid assassins have been mistaken for serial killers over the years."

"Is that where Cam was going?" Matthew asked.

Deets shrugged. "I think he was considering it, yes."

"A hired assassin could change his methods to throw off the police."

"Yes," Deets agreed. "In fact, Cameron speculated on whether two serial killers could actually be the same man."

Alex looked at Matthew. "If the method of killing isn't fixed in the killer's mind. Then the fact that bodies stopped turning up having been killed a certain way doesn't mean the killer was actually caught."

Matthew nodded. "Cam must have believed one of the case study killers might still be out there." He looked at Deets. "Professor, we need to get a copy of that textbook."

Deets stood up and moved over to his desk. He pulled a slim, hard-bound volume out from under a messy pile of papers and handed it to Matthew. "I'll help in any way I can, Mr. Smart. I'm just despondent over poor Cameron's death."

"We'd like to look at Cam's homework too, if we can."

"I'll send everything I have to you."

Matthew handed the professor his business card. "My email address is on there." He shook Deets' hand. "Thank you for your time, Professor. If you think of anything else that might be helpful, please get in touch."

"Of course."

~SC~

Alex dragged herself home a few hours later, her stomach rumbling unhappily and her body sore with weariness. She parked in the small lot behind her apartment building and climbed out, reaching back inside to grab her purse and the box with the baby birds in it. As she moved the box, a chorus of frantic chirping greeted her. "Okay, babies. I'm working on it." She slammed her car door and headed toward the building where she lived. Shadows clutched the sidewalk close and Alex had to look down to make sure she stayed on the concrete. A thin light slipped over her and she looked up at the timid glow of a half-moon high overhead. The meager light was quickly extinguished when clouds slid back over the moon's face.

Her keys jangled as she lifted them to unlock the door.

The sound of a sliding door opening overhead brought Alex's gaze up. The soulful strains of blues music throbbed out into the cool night air. A dark form moved onto the balcony. Something sparked in the low moonlight as the silhouette lifted a hand toward his face. The movement stopped and a man leaned forward, his face illuminated by the lamplight within. "Hey, Alex."

Her hand stopped a foot away from the lock. "Hey, George. How's it goin' today?"

The disembodied face offered a grimace. "Bad day at the office. Two deaths. One of them was a kid."

"Oh, I'm so sorry. I lived in dread of those days." George was interning at the emergency room in nearby St. Joseph's Hospital. They'd bonded with medical school horror stories the first day she'd moved into her place. A fresh barrage of chirping had her lifting a hand in a wave. "I'll see ya later." She inserted her key in the lock and entered a musty smelling entranceway, hurrying up two flights of stairs to her third floor apartment. She was opening her door when she realized she'd forgotten to grab her mail from the wall of boxes in the foyer.

Alex hesitated. Her comfy pjs were calling to her from beyond the door. She could almost taste the spaghetti left overs she was planning to reheat for her dinner. Alex finally decided to grab her mail the next morning on her way out. She pushed the door open, reaching to flick the switch on the wall. The light flickered on, illuminating most of the small one bedroom apartment in a weak, yellow glare. Alex made a mental note to get a better bulb for the overhead light in front of the door.

She dropped her keys onto a small table in the entrance and put her purse down beside them. Alex reached to pull off one shoe and flung it to the tile floor. She took a moment to rub the soreness out of her foot before reaching for the other shoe.

The light in the room shifted slightly and she stopped, lifting her head to peer around the space. From where she stood she could see the entire living space, including the kitchen area. Everything looked just the way she'd left it that morning.

Headlights flickered over the large window that dominated the far wall and she realized she'd probably just seen one of her neighbors turning into the lot. Alex pulled off her second shoe and threw it down, heading toward the kitchen with her chattering baby birds. She settled the box onto the counter and started to turn.

An arm snaked around her throat. Something cool and sharp rested against the soft flesh beneath her chin. "Don't make a sound." The harshly whispered words turned her blood cold as her very active imagination kicked into overdrive. Panic clawed its way through her chest and tightened her lungs, making it hard to breathe. Alex went very still, concentrating on pulling air into her lungs.

The man behind her tightened his grip around her throat and the blade dug into her flesh, sending a jolt of bright pain searing like fire into her. She clamped her lips down on a small, strangled sound of alarm.

Alex engaged her senses, realizing if she lived through the encounter she would need as much information as possible to find the guy. He pulled her up tight against his body and Alex shuddered with revulsion. Despite her best attempts to remain analytical, conscious thought was sheared off under a fresh wave of alarm. The lips that nuzzled her ear were dry…the breath behind them sweet and slightly minty. It was an incongruous thing…that sweetness. She would have expected a man wielding a knife to have sour breath. Shoving the unhelpful thought away, Alex forced herself to focus on the minimal information she could glean. He was taller than her and smelled of sweat. The arm that threatened to choke off her breath was covered in a dusting of golden hair. The wrist was thick, a splotch of black ink showing on the inside curve. She focused on that ink, praying he'd turn his arm so she could get a look at his tat.

"This is a warning, Alex. It's the only one you'll get. Keep your cute little nose out of my business, or you'll find yourself wearing a toe tag like your client."

She stilled, her eyes widening. It wasn't what she'd thought at all. She'd thought he was there to rape her…or at the very least rob her. "I…I have no idea what you're talking about."

The arm tightened and she choked as he applied pressure to her throat. "Shut it!"

Alex's eyes bulged as she struggled to breathe against the pressure on her throat. She wanted to claw at the arm restricting her air but she was all too cognizant of the blade slicing into her tender flesh. Still, as fear turned to full on panic, Alex couldn't stop herself from struggling. Her hands clawed the arm around her throat and even the bright pain of the knife slicing her skin couldn't calm her panic.

But it was no use. He was too strong and she was getting weak. Finally, blackness encroached, spreading inward from the edges of her vision, and she felt herself folding downward as oblivion tugged her into charcoal release.

The last thing she saw as her eyes fluttered closed, was the rigid form of a deadly blade, and the flash of movement as he swung.

# CHAPTER ELEVEN

"The hair from the dent in the black Suburban was a positive for Roberta Snow."

"Really? Good. You're going over the car for DNA evidence?"

"Of course. Unfortunately, since it's a rental it's rife with all kinds of DNA. None of which will be useful unless we find a suspect to match it to."

"Uh-huh." Matthew glanced at the clock on the wall.

"We also ran that license photo you gave us and came up with a match," Detective Hanks told Matthew.

Matthew scratched Max's belly and continued staring at the clock. The little dog's eyes narrowed and he groaned with pleasure. "Okay." Matthew glanced at his watch in the hopes that the clock was wrong and then frowned, his thoughts a million miles away. Alex was late for work. It was very unusual for her, even in the short time she'd worked at Smart Investigations, to be even a minute late. In fact, she was usually early.

"…ex-military with no known address."

Matthew blinked. "Wait. What? Who is it?"

A brief silence met his question. Hanks hated repeating herself. "What's going on, Smart? You're usually not so distracted."

He sighed. "It's Alex. She's late coming in today."

"And that's cause for major concern?"

"Yes. No." He scrubbed a hand over his chin. "I don't know. It's not like her. And after what happened to Cameron…"

"I understand. Why don't I just send you what I have and you can go find your lovely assistant?"

Matthew bristled at the implication. "It has nothing to do with how she looks, Hanks."

"Right. Keep telling yourself that."

The outer office door slammed shut and Matthew's head jerked up. "There she is. Send me that stuff. And thanks." He hung up and stood. Max left his bed and hopped into Matthew's chair, jumping to the floor from there. He trotted after Matthew, his fringe of a tail wagging enthusiastically. But when he reached the doorway, Max's tail drooped.

If Matthew'd had a tail, his would have drooped too.

John Snow stood beside Alex's desk, perusing the papers scattered over its surface. His broad shoulders were stooped and his jaw was set. He'd just started to reach for Alex's notebook when Matthew stepped into the outer office. "Mr. Snow." He offered his new client his hand. "What can I do for you?"

The man's pale blue gaze slid over Matthew and around the room. "No assistant today?"

Matthew fought to keep his expression neutral. He was surprised Snow even mentioned Alex, since he'd done everything he could to ignore her the last time he'd been in the office. "She's running a little late. Would you like an update of our investigation so far?"

Snow nodded. "Yes. Please." His hands clenched at his sides but he seemed to forcibly unclench them, shoving them into the pockets of his slacks. "I feel so useless…just waiting around." He shook his head. "I wish I could do more."

Matthew set aside his worry about Alex for a moment and allowed himself to feel his client's pain. "I'm so sorry, Mr. Snow. I know it must be very hard for you. Maybe if I tell you about our progress it will help."

The man nodded and, when Matthew indicated his office, preceded him in and sat down. Max trotted over to his second bed, the one on the floor under the window. When there were clients in the office, he wasn't allowed in the tiny bed on Matthew's desk.

Under the little dog's watchful eye, Snow ran a hand over his bristly chin and sighed. Looking at Snow across his desk, Matthew realized how tired the man looked. His eyes were puffy with purple slashes underneath. Picking up his cell, Matthew smiled. "Just give me one minute. I need to send a quick text." He typed out a short text to Alex to call him and then forced himself to turn to the matter in front of him.

"Now, Mr. Snow, here's what we've learned so far…" He quickly updated his new client on the discovery at the Quick Stop, the possible mistake with the skid marks, the eyewitness testimonies and the discovery of the dented car at Bashin' Jack's. "We went to the address the man provided and found out he'd been staying in an abandoned building."

Snow frowned. "A homeless guy?"

Matthew nodded. "It appears that way, yes."

"But why would a homeless guy kill my daughter?"

"If he did kill her…we still haven't verified that…"

"Come on, Smart. Don't be dense. Of course he killed her. All the evidence points to it."

Matthew lifted a hand to stop him. "It appears that he killed her. But I'm not done with my investigation and I'm reserving judgement until I am."

Snow's face was dark with rage, but he looked away, visibly working to regain calm. "Fair enough," he finally said. "What do you know about this guy?"

"Actually, the police are sending over what they have

on him today. If there's anything there that helps me find him, I'll let you know right away."

Snow nodded and stood, offering Matthew his hand. "Thank you for your help, Mr. Smart. I know I'm a bit emotional right now..."

Matthew shook his head. "Perfectly understandable. We're going to do everything in our power to find out what happened, Mr. Snow. You have my word on that."

"Good." He started toward the door and stopped, turning back. "I hope your assistant's okay. Alex, was it? I didn't get the impression she was the type to be late."

The niggle of concern that had been eating away at him in the background during his discussion with Snow slammed over him in full force. Matthew simply nodded and watched his client stride out of the office his gut churning.

~SC~

The first thing she became aware of was the pain. It was like a living force, pounding against the inside of her skull trying to get out.

Pound, pound, pound, pound.

Alex groaned, squeezing her eyes tighter against the rays of sunlight bathing the room in light. She'd had a rough night. Not only had she suffered the mother of all headaches, she'd lain in terror for hours after coming to on the floor of her kitchen.

When she'd finally succumbed to exhaustion around dawn, nightmares had kept her on the edge of wakefulness, every sound feeding into the terrors of her battered brain to make sleep almost less restful than being awake.

Alex pressed shaky fingers into her temples, trying to still the incessant pounding. It didn't help much, at least not long term, the pounding returned with a vengeance as soon as she stopped.

In the distance somebody's dog was barking...a

constant, incessant intrusion on her misery. Alex wanted to put a pillow over her head and drown out the noise. Just another hour of sleep. That was all she needed to gain a clear head. Maybe the tortuous pounding in her head would finally go away if she got enough sleep.

"Alex! Open the door!"

Her eyes shot open. The pounding she'd thought was inside her head was actually coming from the front of her apartment. And the barking...

Alex sat up too fast and agony sliced furrows into her brain. She cried out, holding her head as she took deep breaths until the worst of it passed.

"Alex!"

She tried to call out to Matthew but the words got caught in her throat and came out sounding like the croak of a bullfrog. She shoved herself out of bed and shuffled to the door, clearing her throat and swallowing the frog. "I'm coming. Hold on."

Blessed relief. The pounding and barking stopped. Alex unlocked the door and dragged it open before remembering how she was dressed...

Max flew into the apartment and threw himself against her legs, whining. She reached down and scratched his fuzzy little head, stooping down to pick him up before she remembered it was a bad idea. "Oh god!" She put a hand over her face and rode out the pain. When she opened her eyes again, she discovered Max's owner was standing very close, swamping her in heat and his delicious sandalwood scent.

Matthew's eyes were filled with worry. Until he took a gander at her outfit. Then they were filled with something else entirely.

Too sick and sore to feel the embarrassment she should have felt opening the door to her boss wearing only her boy style panties and a tank top with no bra, Alex turned away from the door and stumbled toward the kitchen. It wasn't until she reached for the handle of the refrigerator, suddenly desperate for the cool sweetness of a glass of orange juice that she realized she was clutching her derringer in one hand.

"Alex, what happened to you?" Matthew was suddenly there, his hand lifting to touch her temple. She grabbed his hand before he touched the spot where the intruder had punched her. "It's okay. I'm fine."

At the sound of Alex's voice, the baby birds started chirping loudly.

"You're not fine. You have a fist-sized bruise on your temple and you're carrying a gun. Tell me what happened." Matthew grabbed the baggie of crushed bugs she'd placed next to the box and fed the babies while Alex poured herself a glass of juice and downed it.

Her eyes closed with pleasure as the cool liquid soothed her throat. "Thank you. Poor things haven't been fed for hours."

"What happened, Alex?" His voice held a warning note. He was losing patience.

"I'll tell you everything. Just, give me a minute. I had a rough night and my head is killing me."

"Of course it's killing you. You need to go to the hospital."

She shook her head and then sucked air as her brain bounced painfully around in her skull. "No hospital. I just need some aspirin."

"I'll get them. Where?"

She pointed to her bedroom and then, suddenly unable to stand a moment longer, sank to the floor and pulled Max onto her lap. He wriggled happily as she hugged him close, his sweet, canine scent and softness soothing her jangled nerves.

A moment later Matthew handed her three extra strength pain killers and a glass of water. She downed them and then settled Max on the floor and stood, with Matthew's help. "When I got home last night someone was in the apartment waiting for me."

Matthew's sexy caramel-brown gaze widened. "Oh my god!" He took a step closer, reaching to touch her face with a warm finger. "He didn't…"

She shook her head, relieved to find the pain killers were working. Her brain didn't slosh around in her head quite as much. "He was apparently here to give me a warning."

"What kind of warning?"

"He told me to keep my nose out of his business or I'd be dead like my client." She lifted her gaze to Matthew's, the import of the warning hitting her full force. "He knew my name, Matthew." To her horror, tears burned in her eyes.

As soon as he saw them the rage in his face fell away and he reached for her, pulling her into the safe harbor of his big, hard form. "It's okay, Alex. We'll get to the bottom of this. I won't let this guy hurt you again."

# CHAPTER TWELVE

Alex had barely slept in days. She'd poured over the case studies in Cam's textbook and extracted the two that were most likely to be the cause of his focus. Then she'd asked Detective Hanks to locate all known cases for the two killers. Working pretty much day and night, Alex had reviewed the findings and pulled out as much information as she could gather on the victims, the killer's methods and background. She was typing each case up into its own discovery report and then she would offer them to Hanks in the hopes she could match something, anything current to one of them.

The words on her computer screen blurred and Alex stopped typing, closing her eyes against the weariness dragging her down. A steaming mug appeared in front of her and she looked up at Matthew, smiling gratefully. The coffee was hot and dark just like she liked it. Taking a sip, she closed her eyes and sighed. "Perfect. Thank you."

"Where are the birds?" Matthew asked.

"I let them go this morning." She grinned. "I decided they were ready when they flew over to the bookshelf without crashing."

"That's great. Good job, mama. Now maybe you can

get the bugs out of your teeth."

Alex grinned. "Ha, ha."

Matthew stood watching her work for a moment and then reached out to rub her shoulders. She tensed at first and then gave in to the delicious warmth and soothing touch. "Oh god, that feels good."

"You need to get some rest, Alex. You're going to make yourself sick."

She shook her head and took another sip from her mug. "I'm almost done." She placed a hand on the keyboard again and he reached out, pulling it away. "I'm insisting. The work will still be here in the morning."

She frowned, clasping the mug in one hand like a lifeline. Alarm swirled through her. He was going to make her go home. "I'm not tired. Really."

Matthew closed her laptop and picked it up. He sat down on her desk, facing her. "You left tired behind days ago. Now you're exhausted."

She gave a quick shake of her head and hid behind the mug. Fragrant steam bathed her face, making her eyes drift helplessly closed. She jerked them open and set the mug down so she wouldn't drop it. He was right. She could barely keep her eyes open. But the idea of going back to her apartment...

Alex forced a smile. "How about if I just catch a quick nap on the couch in your office? You can go on home. I'll be fine."

Matthew stood up, settled the computer back onto her desk, and reached for her. He pulled her to her feet and grabbed her purse from the small table behind her desk. Shoving it into her arms, he wrapped an arm around her shoulders and led her toward the door. "I know you're scared to sleep at your apartment, Alex."

She shook her head. "No, I..."

Matthew placed a finger over her lips. The clean scent of his skin teased her and she fought the temptation to distract him from his mission with a kiss. "It's okay to be scared. You don't have to be Wonder Woman." He whistled for Max. The soft thud of the tiny dog's paws hitting Matthew's chair and then again as he landed on the floor was followed by the soft click of nails across the wood floor. A beat later Max bounced from the office and ran to Alex. The little dog lifted to his hind feet and whined softly, begging for her to pick him up.

"That's why Max and I are going to sleep on your couch tonight."

Alex stopped in the middle of lifting Max, her eyes widening. "Oh, I couldn't ask you to do that."

Matthew opened the exterior door and flipped off the lights. He ushered her through before him and stopped to engage the security alarm and locks. "It's a good thing you didn't then. I offered." He grinned as Max bathed her face lovingly, making her laugh. "Max insists. He's been worried about you."

The grin slid away and Alex looked up into Matthew's eyes. Unmistakable heat flared in their depths. He was suddenly close. Too close. Bathing her in heat from his big, hard body. Alex pulled air slowly into her lungs, fighting for calm as her senses exploded into awareness.

They stood there for a long moment, inches apart, and Matthew's gaze slid to her mouth. She stilled, like a deer fixed in a rifle scope. He moved an infinitesimal amount but it was enough to make her sexual core tighten as his breath bathed her face in heat.

He was going to kiss her. Alex knew it with the certainty of a woman who'd been subconsciously memorizing everything about the man she wanted.

But he seemed to shake himself out of the trance and he nodded toward the stairs. "Let's go. We'll stop for burgers on the way to your place and then home."

She let him steer her toward the stairwell, her mind racing. She was terrified to go home alone. But if she was honest she was even more terrified of going there with him. "What about Max? You don't have his food."

"He can eat a burger too."

She started down the stairs, Max's warm little head resting sweetly and trustingly on her shoulder. "But you don't have clothes. Or a toothbrush."

His smile was slow and knowing. She flushed, realizing he'd caught her trying to come up with excuses not to let him into her home. He was a very smart man and he'd know why she was making those excuses. "I have a bag in the car. I never know when I'll need to head out of town last minute on a case."

She bit back a sigh. Beaten. "Okay, but if you're going to give up your bed for me, I can at least take Max off your hands. I have a feeling he'll hog the couch."

Max lifted his head and swiped his soft tongue along her jaw.

Matthew's lips twitched. "Thank you for making the ultimate sacrifice. I know it will be a hardship for you."

She finally broke into a grin. "Don't mention it. I'm happy to take one for the team."

~SC~

Hanks called Matthew as they were trudging up the stairs to Alex's apartment. "Hey," he answered, "what's up?"

"I might have found your guy."

Matthew's eyes widened. He put out a hand to stop Alex. "I'm listening."

"We picked your vagrant up on a loitering charge. I told the officers not to tell him any more than that. Do you want to talk to him?"

"I'll be right down." He disconnected and turned to Alex. "I need to go down to the station. Hanks found our homeless guy."

Alex nodded and started down the stairs. Matthew put a hand on her arm to stop her. "You should stay here with Max. You're dead on your feet."

She shook her head. "Food revived me. I'm fine.

There's no way I'm missing this interview."

He frowned, casting an assessing gaze over her face. Despite the circles under her pretty eyes, she did look better. "Okay. Come on. Hopefully you can tell me if it's the guy who attacked you."

She trotted down the steps behind him, Max still cuddled close in her arms. Matthew held the door for her. "You'll have to stay in the observation room with Max. He can't go into the interview room anyway and I don't want this guy to get a look at you."

She frowned but nodded. Apparently the attack in her apartment had spooked her enough to encourage her to be sensible. That was good. Because he had no intention of letting her face off with the killer alone again.

Or at all if he could help it.

~SC~

The man the police knew as Gregg Pence sat unblinking beneath the stark florescent light, staring straight ahead. He was gaunt and filthy, his beard and hair tangled with debris. He looked like he'd been sleeping on the ground somewhere.

Hanks handed Matthew a file. "That's everything we have on Pence. It's not much. He was in the military or we wouldn't have that. He has no surviving family. Last known residence was in Gary, Indiana. The house has since been demolished to make way for a shopping center." Hanks stared at the man through the one way glass and frowned. "He was honorably discharged in 2013 and then fell off the radar until he was brought into St. Joseph's with frostbite and alcohol poisoning. They assumed he'd tried to drink himself warm." She shook her head. "Too many of our military heroes end up this way."

"PTSD?" Alex asked.

Hanks looked her way. "Probably. Though he's never been tested. He snuck out of St. Joseph's before anyone could talk to him about therapy." She shrugged. "He's been off our radar since then."

"Where'd you find him?" Matthew asked.

"Over by campus. He has a refrigerator box stuck in the middle of a copse of evergreens at the back of the property. Nobody even knew he was there."

"Anything connect him to Roberta Snow?"

"Or her father?" Alex added.

"Not that we can find. But I'd say it's too much of a coincidence that he's former military."

Matthew nodded. "I intend to ask my client about him as soon as possible."

"Somebody paid him a lot of money recently," Hanks told them. "We found five hundred dollars in small bills in his pockets."

"Credit cards? Driver's license?"

Detective Hanks glanced toward Matthew. "No. If he's the guy from Bashin' Jack's he got rid of the document trail."

Matthew sighed. "Shall we go see what we can find out?"

"Let's do it."

Matthew stopped in front of Alex as Hanks opened the door and moved through it into the Interview room. He leaned close, speaking softly. "Anything about him seem familiar?"

She shook her head. "I need to hear him talk."

"Okay." He gave her a reassuring smile. "You're safe here."

"I know." The smile she gave him back was slightly brittle. Alex was a strong woman, but she wasn't stupid. The man who'd attacked her had known where she lived. He'd managed to get into her place without her knowing. And he'd known her name and what they were working on. He wasn't just some street thug. And they needed to tread very carefully until they figured out who he was.

Matthew patted her arm and followed Hanks through the door. She was sitting across from the homeless man, speaking in soft tones to him. But Pence didn't seem to hear her. His gaze was fixed on the long mirror across from him. The one way glass that shielded Alex from the room. Almost as if he knew she was there.

"Mr. Pence." Matthew offered the man his hand and it was ignored. He dropped it to his side and sat down next to Hanks. "My name is Matthew Smart. I've been hired to find out what happened to a young woman named Roberta Snow. Do you know the name?"

Pence stared mutely ahead, his body perfectly, unnaturally still.

"Miss Snow was hit by a rented Suburban when she was out jogging," Matthew tried again. "We have records showing that you recently rented a similar car from Bashin' Jack's car rentals."

Pence didn't respond.

Hanks and Matthew shared a look. Finally Hanks leaned forward. "Mr. Pence, we have evidence that you rented the car that hit Miss Snow. This is your chance to tell your side of the story."

Pence slowly turned his head, fixing a cold hazel gaze on Matthew. "You went to the house. Sent a doctor to Sydney."

Matthew stilled, unsure how to respond. He didn't know who Sydney was and certainly hadn't sent any doctors to anyone. But then he remembered Alex saying something about a friend who was a doctor. He decided to go with the assumption she'd followed up on her promise to the homeless woman. "Yes. My friend did. Is Sydney better?"

Pence pursed his lips, the cracks in the neglected skin filled with dirt. "Yes. She's better."

"Good. That's good."

"I didn't drive that car."

Matthew blinked at the change in topic. "You didn't?"

"No."

"You rented it for someone else?" Hanks asked.

"Yes."

Matthew and Hanks shared a look. "Who was it?"

Pence shrugged.

"You rented a car for a man you didn't know?" Hanks asked, clearly unconvinced.

Pence shrugged again. His gaze slipped back to the mirror, fixed on the reflection there, and he remained silent.

Matthew decided it was time to change tacks. "You met a man on the street and he offered you money to rent the car."

Pence's gaze slid his way briefly and then returned to the mirror.

Matthew took that as affirmation and went on. "The man gave you a credit card and driver's license for a new name and sent you into Bashin' Jack's. You rented the car and walked out of the lot. The man came back later and took the car."

"I didn't want to hurt those people."

Cindy scanned Matthew another look. "What people?"

"The man scared easy." Pence frowned. "I wouldn't hurt the woman. He wanted me to. I told him I don't like to hurt women."

"What woman?"

Pence shrugged and stared at the mirror.

"Did you follow a woman to her home and hit her?"

"I told you. I don't hurt women. I told him the same thing."

"How?" Hanks asked. "How did you tell him? Did you meet?"

"The concrete river. Where the fat letters dance."

Realizing it was probably worse than useless, given the man was talking nonsense, Matthew pressed him for more information. "What does the man who paid you look like?" he asked. "Did he give you a name?"

"Like me. Nameless, faceless. Nobody sees us."

Matthew expelled a frustrated breath. "Can you give us

anything that might help us find him, Mr. Pence. A woman's life depends on it."

Pence dragged his gaze away from the mirror and fixed a suddenly sharp gaze on Matthew. "He had dead eyes. Cold and cruel."

They asked Pence questions for another hour but he said nothing more that was useful. Reluctantly, Matthew left Hanks to finish up and re-entered the observation room. He found Alex pacing, her fists clenched and her gaze on fire. She turned on him as he entered the room. "That bastard had me followed by a crazy man. I could have been killed."

"We don't know that for sure. But I agree it's a possibility. Did you recognize Pence's voice?"

"No. That's not him. I'm guessing whoever paid him to rent the car for him was the one who attacked me in my home." She fixed Matthew with an angry gaze. "We need to find this guy, Matthew. Before he hurts someone else."

"Yes. We do. But to do that we first need to figure out what his goal is."

She grabbed a sleeping Max out of a nearby chair. "I have a better idea. Why don't we just go ask him?"

Matthew felt his eyes go wide. "You know where he is?"

She pulled the door open and stormed through, into the hallway. Hanks was just closing the door to the Interview Room. She looked up when Matthew joined Alex in the hall.

He grabbed Alex's arm. "Hold on. Talk to me, Alex. Where are we going?"

She looked at him like he had two heads. "Really? You didn't get that?"

He shook his head. "Enlighten me."

"The concrete river? Dancing letters. That doesn't ring any bells?"

He felt himself losing patience. "Alex…"

She looked at Hanks. "The canal. The bridges are

covered in street art. Our guy must have met Pence somewhere along the canal downtown."

"Of course!" Hanks agreed. "I'll get some officers in place to watch it." She fixed Alex with a look. "You need to stay away from there until we find out why this guy was having you watched."

Matthew and Alex shared a guilty look. "I think we already know that," Matthew offered. "Well, we kind of know but we're not exactly sure why he targeted Alex."

Hanks skimmed a glare between them. "Talk to me. What have you been holding back?"

Alex frowned. "It's my fault. I begged him not to tell you. I didn't want it blown up into a thing."

"It's already a thing, Alex," Matthew said, exasperated by his part in not telling the police. "I should have told you, Cindy. Maybe she would have felt safer with police protection…"

The detective sighed. "Just tell me, Matthew."

He quickly filled her in on Alex's terrifying experience from a few nights earlier. She expelled a harsh breath when he'd finished. "So we know why he was having her followed, but not why he targeted her."

"Exactly. It's my company," Matthew argued. "My investigation. Alex has only been working with me for a few days. It makes no sense to threaten her instead of me."

"Unless he assumed I'd be the weaker link," Alex offered.

"But he'd have to believe I'd stop investigating Roberta Snow's death because you asked me to. That's a leap."

"Unless it wasn't about Roberta Snow," Detective Hanks offered.

Matthew and Alex both turned confused expressions her way. "What else would it be about?" Matthew asked.

Hanks lifted a light brown eyebrow. "What else are you investigating right now?"

Alex gasped, turning to Matthew. "Cam's murder. He's trying to scare me into quitting my job. Whatever Cam was investigating, this guy must have had something to do with it."

"And he's afraid you'll find something that would set you on his trail," Matthew scrubbed a hand over his jaw. "That actually makes sense."

"Yeah." Alex agreed. "Now we just need to figure out what Cam was investigating."

# CHAPTER THIRTEEN

Alex had to force herself to climb the steps to her place. She was so tired she stumbled twice, inspiring Matthew to wrap a big, warm hand around her arm. Not wanting him to see her as weak, she tried to pull away. "I'm okay."

Matthew didn't let her loose. "You're more than okay. But you're so tired I'm afraid you'll tumble right down these stairs and just go to sleep at the bottom."

She was even too tired to smile. "Not a bad idea at all."

He chuckled. Taking the keys from her hand, Matthew inserted the correct one into her lock and pushed the door open. "Off to bed. No arguing."

She flashed him a droopy salute and stumbled toward her darkened bedroom. Sitting down on the edge of her bed, Alex toed off her shoes and dropped backward, barely able to stay awake long enough to tug the covers back.

As she was drifting off to sleep, she was vaguely aware of someone pulling the sheet and comforter up to her chin, followed by a gentle burrowing that ended with a warm little body snuggled against her hip.

She was pretty sure she smiled as her hand found Max's

silky fur. But then the world disappeared behind a charcoal curtain. And she gave herself over to sleep.

She must have slept deeply for a while, because sometime later she wove the heat of a late morning sun into her nightmare when it began. In her dream, she was standing beside the canal, staring into the water. Something swirled on the black water's surface and she stepped closer to look at it. The oily substance turned red as she dropped to one knee, her hand reaching for the shape beginning to emerge at the bottom. Despite an unwillingness to touch the ribbon of red swirling on the water's surface, Alex plunged her hand through the oily liquid just as the unformed shadows at the murky bottom rose toward her. A large hand, fingers square and tanned as they wrapped around hers, squeezed her flesh and tugged as a face with no features broke the surface of the water. Dark eyes narrowed with rage and she lost her balance, starting to fall. Before she hit the water, a familiar voice said her name.

Stay out of my business. Or you're gonna end up dead too.

Movement flashed and the image of a knife brought a scream to her lips as the bloody water flew toward her face. She jerked upright, her terrified gaze sliding around the sun-drenched bedroom. The covers next to her rose up and danced as Max made his way out from his warm nest with his tail wagging. He climbed into her lap and licked her fingers as she fought to calm her racing heart.

The bedroom door opened. Matthew stood there, his thick blond hair tangled from sleep and his sexy beard slightly disheveled. His gaze was filled with concern. "Are you all right? I heard you cry out."

She scooped Max up and pulled him close, burying her face in his sweet-smelling fur. "I'm okay. Just a nightmare."

Matthew scrubbed a hand through his hair, sending it even further into disarray. "I'll make coffee."

Alex nodded and blinked as an image from her nightmare flared up again in her memory. She surged to her feet and Max yelped in surprise. "Wait!"

Matthew stilled in the doorway. "What is it?" Whatever he saw in her face had him moving toward her, his handsome face filled with worry. "What's wrong, Alex?"

She grabbed the hand he stretched toward her, clasping it in her icy grip. "I remembered something from the attack." Excitement flared through her. "He had a tattoo on his wrist. It was a knife with a jagged blade and a twisted hilt."

Matthew's eyes widened. "Can you draw it?"

"I think so."

Matthew pulled her toward the kitchen. "Let's do it then. We'll have Hanks search the known criminal database for a match." He stopped, turning to her with a sparkle in his caramel brown eyes. "This could be the break we need, Alex."

His excitement was infectious. She nodded, a grin spreading across her face. "I know."

He stared down at her a moment longer, something unreadable in his gaze, and then suddenly gave her hand a tug, pulling her into his arms. Before she could even form a thought, Matthew's lips were on hers and heat was exploding in her belly. She made a faint sound of pure need, her hands coming up to frame his square jaw. The soft bristles of his beard tickled the palms of her hands and she rubbed them as his lips played over hers, sending her senses into overdrive.

A small part of Alex's mind told her she had to stop…they had no business doing what they were doing…but he felt so big and hot and delicious pressed against her and his lips were so gentle and sweet. Still, reality was bound to intrude on the fantasy she knew she could never indulge. Max barked, bumping against Matthew's leg in a not so subtle bid for breakfast. Matthew broke the kiss on a sigh. He rubbed her lips with his thumb as he rested his forehead against hers. "I'm sorry. I know I shouldn't have done that." He lifted his head and fixed her with an intense gaze. "It's not right and I know that. It's just that I…" He sighed again. "I've been wanting to do that since you first walked into the office."

Alex tried not to be disappointed. After all, she'd been thinking exactly the same thing. But that kiss hadn't been just a random touch of lips. It had been fire and dynamite and promise all rolled into one. She nodded, stepping away and shoving her tangled hair off her face. "It's okay. Just make sure it doesn't happen again."

His gaze darkened slightly and she realized she'd disappointed him too. She told herself that was as it should be. They could never act on what they felt for each other. Not as long as they worked together. And Alex really wanted to keep her job at Smart Investigations. "I'll make us some coffee and feed Max while you do the sketch. We can drop it off to Cindy on the way to the canal."

"Sure. Okay."

She watched him walk away, the tiny dog dancing at his heels, and decided the day which had showed so much promise a moment earlier, had lost a good bit of its luster when he left.

~SC~

They sat at her kitchen table, Alex picking at her eggs.

"You don't like your breakfast?" Matthew scanned a look over her and wasn't happy with what he saw. She looked tired, with purple arcs beneath her startling eyes. And the bruise on her temple from the attack days earlier stood out against her too-pale skin.

She looked up, seemingly surprised by his question. "I'm sorry." She settled her fork onto her plate, pushing it away. "I'm not really hungry." She sipped her coffee, the slim arcs of her brows furrowing in thought.

Matthew stood up and took her plate, putting it on the floor for Max to clean. "What is it? You've been thinking way too hard since you woke up? Is it your nightmare?"

Alex shoved a thick strand of shiny hair off her cheek. "No. Well, not exactly. I just keep thinking about the water and the symbolism." Her gaze slid up, fixed on his. "I want to go to the canal. Will you come with me?"

He blinked in surprise at her request. Not that she wanted to go, but that she wanted him with her. He'd been afraid he'd lost her trust with that kiss. A kiss he couldn't find it within himself to regret. "Of course. Are you looking for something specific?"

"I'll know when I get there." She stood. "Give me twenty minutes and I'll be ready to go."

Matthew watched her walk away, his gaze sliding over her with guilty appreciation. She was one of the smartest people he knew…and one of the most delicious women he'd ever met.

He nearly groaned aloud at the thought. He was lost. And he had no idea how he was going to keep his promise to Alex never to pursue her delectable lips again. Just the thought of that kiss…her lush, soft body pressing against his…robbed him of breath and thought.

If he didn't pull himself together, he was going to be nearly worthless in the work ahead.

~SC~

Later they sat in silence on the drive to the precinct. Matthew felt uncomfortable about kissing her and she seemed deep in thought. The shrill sound of ringing finally burst the silence between them. Matthew looked at the name on the screen and sighed.

"Trouble?" Alex frowned.

"Big trouble." He hit Ignore on the call. "Do you have family, Alex?"

Her smile was soft. "Two sisters and a brother. We were raised by my mom."

"I'm sorry. What happened to your dad?"

She turned away, glancing out the window as if she

were uncomfortable with the question.

Matthew lifted his hands. "I don't mean to pry…"

"No. It's fine. I'm just missing them is all." She turned back to him, her expression sad. "My dad left when he found out mama was pregnant with me. She never remarried, which is a shame because she's a beautiful, smart, funny lady."

"Having met her daughter, I have zero doubt that's true."

Alex shook her head but the ghost of a smile found her face. "My father apparently told her he didn't want any more kids. Then I happened. He considered me too big a mistake to forgive."

"That's ridiculous, Alex—"

To his amazement, she laughed. "Don't think I let his opinion of me color my world view because I don't. My mother made it clear to me all my life that I was the best thing to ever happen to her. I apparently freed her from a loveless marriage and she was proud of raising us kids alone. She did a great job as a single parent and I know it was far from easy. But mama always told me I could do or be anything I wanted and I believed her."

"Where are they now? Your family?"

Living in Southern Indiana. In a small town called Crocker. It's beautiful but there aren't a lot of opportunities for someone with my background." Shrugging, she said, "I see them on holidays and stuff…"

"I'd like to meet them."

Genuine warmth filled her sexy gaze. "I'd like that too. But you'd better watch out for my youngest sister. She's a man-hunting shark with pretty eyes."

Matthew laughed. "She should meet my sister. Tandy would probably put your sister to shame in the man-hunting department."

A spark of humor joined the warmth in her gaze. "My money's on Bethy. I feel it's only safe to warn you. Your sister doesn't have a chance in this contest."

"We'll see." Matthew laughed, shaking his head. "It could be the clash of the Titans."

~SC~

An hour later they walked onto the walking and biking trail that lined both sides of the canal in downtown Indianapolis. Matthew spotted one of Hank's men and stopped for a moment to speak with him. Max ran over to the young cop, tail wagging, and jumped up on his leg to get the requisite quota of adoration. Crouched low to scratch Max under the chin and behind the ears, Officer Devan Tremwell told Matthew that the police had assigned plain clothes teams to watch the canal throughout the day and night, but they hadn't seen anyone yet who matched the admittedly weak description Pence had given them.

"You mean you haven't seen a single homeless guy with cold, dead eyes?" Matthew joked.

Tremwell shook his head, straightening. "We're not sure what we're looking for, but I promise we're looking as hard as we can." He grinned.

When Matthew turned away from the cop, he realized Alex had wandered down the canal and stood staring into the water. She was near a bridge, the concrete walls behind her rich with urban art, and he thought for a moment that she'd found the meeting spot.

His pulse pounding, Matthew tugged Max away from officer Tremwell and hurried toward Alex, his gaze skimming the surrounding area.

He was thirty feet away when she turned to look at him. She smiled, her gaze warming, and he relaxed. Something coughed softly in the distance and Alex jerked, looking down as red blossomed high on her chest.

It took a beat for Matthew to realize what had happened. By then it was too late for him to get to her. She started to wobble, her legs buckling out from under her, and Matthew screamed her name as she toppled sideways into the water of the canal.

# CHAPTER FOURTEEN

The icy water hit her like a fist as she tumbled downward. Alex's pulse pounded in her ears, her heart thumping against her ribs. She'd been shot! She was so stunned she didn't know what to do at first. Pain throbbed dully where she'd been hit and ribbons of red floated brightly upward from the wound.

Her body settled to the slimy bottom of the canal and her hand landed on something that felt like hair. She screamed, brackish water streaming between her lips as something crashed above her and a large form cut the dark water in her direction.

That was when she realized she needed to swim, but her arms and legs wouldn't cooperate and her thoughts were growing increasingly muzzy. Something was wrong.

Something was horribly wrong.

Her lungs screamed with the need for air and Alex had to clamp down on the urge to inhale. But when she tried to reason out why she couldn't breathe, coherent thought danced away, elusive and weak.

The water swayed against her, growing warmer with every brush against her nerveless flesh. Sleep called to her. Sweet oblivion. Alex thought maybe she would just close her eyes for a beat. Take a tiny nap. And when she woke up, she'd figure out what to do next. In the deep recesses of her mind, she knew there was a fatal flaw in that reasoning. But she was just so tired…

A ribbon of cold bitterness slipped between her lips, sliding down her throat, and Alex's eyes dropped closed.

The water buffeted against her, sweeping her across the slimy bottom. Her fingers twitched, getting caught in something soft and tangled. There was a flash of movement and a large shape reared up before her, encompassed her in hard heat, and compelled her upward, toward the light above.

She was vaguely aware of shouting. Barking. Sunlight touched her skin, followed by a cool breeze that made her shiver. Alex's lungs felt like they'd been hardened to lead and she couldn't find a way to pull air into them.

"Breathe, Alex." Gentle hands laid her down onto rough heat and turned her to her side, pressing against her back. "Come on, baby, cough it out and breathe."

A small, warmth nestled into her belly and a soft whine infused her senses, joining with the husky tones of a worried male voice to draw her back.

She coughed and water spewed from between her lips. She coughed again, so violently she retched as it wracked her form.

"That's my girl." Hot hands smoothed over her brow. The whining moved closer and a soft warmth slipped over her cheek.

"Give her some room, Max."

Alex's lips moved and formed around the word, "Max." She wanted so badly to wrap her arms around the tiny dog, enfolding his quivering form in a hug that would anchor her to the world as her mind tried to send her floating above it. But her arms wouldn't move.

Voices throbbed and floated above her.

Is she all right?

I don't know. Hard arms slipped beneath her legs,

under her shoulders. Did you call an ambulance?

It's on its way. I sent someone after the shooter.

You won't find him. A strong, too-fast heartbeat pounded against her ear as her savior pulled her into his arms and started walking. We need to get her out of sight.

What's that clutched in her hand?

I'm guessing it's the thing the shooter didn't want her to find.

Sirens. Barking.

Hush, Max.

The sirens grew ever closer until the sound twanged against her nerves like an off-key symphony. The wailing stopped and metal groaned against metal. Quick, heavy footsteps moved closer, followed by a soft growl.

No, Max. They're trying to help.

Get her on the gurney.

We're coming along too.

Fine. Just get her on the gurney and let's get her to the hospital.

Then the damnable sirens again. She shrank against the delicious softness beneath her head, squeezing her eyes more tightly closed. And let the world slip into blessed silence.

~SC~

Alex looked so pale lying there. Matthew thought he might have lost ten years watching her get shot and fall into that canal. If he hadn't gotten there when he had...

She stirred and opened her eyes, blinking against the light behind his head. "Hey." Matthew reached around and shut off the lamp. "It's about time you woke up, sleepyhead."

She frowned, trying to sit up. "What happened? Why am I in the hospital?"

He wrapped a hand around her arm, stopping her. "Just stay there and let your body catch up to your mind. You were hit with a pretty hefty dose of drugs and there's going to be some residual fog and achiness."

She lay back on her pillow and rubbed her eyes. "Drugs?"

He held up the dart they'd pulled from her shoulder. The fluffy red fibers had been the thing that had horrified him at first glance as she fell. He'd thought it was blood blooming on her chest. Matthew swallowed hard at the memory. He couldn't remember ever having been that scared. "You were darted. I'm guessing he drugged you with a mix of Ketamine and Xylazine or something similar. Your muscles are going to be sore." He sat down in the chair beside the bed and leaned forward, resting a hand over hers. "Do you remember what happened?"

She took a shaky breath. "I remember arriving at the canal. Walking along the water and then…" She frowned. "It's a blank."

He nodded. "Not surprising."

She half turned toward him, grimacing at the movement. "Who shot me?"

"We don't know for sure. The police are looking for the spot where the shooter was standing now. Hopefully someone saw something that will help us." He wrapped his hand around hers, his gaze widening at the coolness of her soft skin. Matthew tugged the extra blanket lying across the foot of the bed up to cover her. "I'm guessing it's our killer. The only question is why?"

She swallowed as if her throat were still tight. "You mean why he didn't kill me?"

Matthew handed her a glass of water. "Unless he didn't know what he was doing…which seems highly unlikely…the cocktail he used in the dart slowed you down, made you loopy and your limbs heavy, but it wasn't fatal. If you hadn't fallen into the canal you would have just been a bit sloggy and slow."

Her gaze widened. "I fell into the canal?" She wrinkled her nose. "Ish! I hope I've been sanitized."

Matthew grimaced at the memory. "There's really a lot

of stuff in the bottom of that thing."

She lifted a hand. "Do me a favor and don't tell me. I'm glad I can't remember."

Matthew's smile widened. "I'm afraid I have to tell you part of it. You came up clutching a fake beard wrapped around a rock to keep it submerged."

Her eyes widened. "Seriously?"

"The lab is checking it right now to see if there's any helpful DNA on it."

"I guess it could just be a coincidence."

"Yeah. But I doubt it. You were staring at the spot where the beard was when you were shot. It's possible the killer was trying to keep you from seeing it. Maybe distract us from our search." Matthew shook his head. "But you fell into the canal and came up with it."

"Does it look like our suspect's beard? The guy from the security video at Bashin' Jack's?"

"I want to look at the video again but I'm thinking it's a very close match. It's possible you found our suspect's disguise. At least part of it."

She nodded. "Then I'm almost glad I fell into the canal." Her nose twitched with obvious disgust.

Matthew was strangely charmed. "If that was his beard, your falling in was a spot of bad luck that might be the end of him."

"I hope so." Her eyes drooped and he realized between the nights of sleeplessness and the drug's effects, she had to be exhausted. He stood and she forced her eyes back open. "I'll get out of here and let you sleep. The doc said you can go home as soon as you feel like it."

Alex made as if to sit up again. "I'm ready now."

"No you're not. But I'll tell you what. You get a few hours' sleep and I'll come back for you around dinner time. We'll get you home and you can have a long, hot shower."

She moaned softly, her eyes already falling closed. "You sweet talker you…"

Matthew stood there for a moment and watched her sleep, unwilling to leave her side. He was jerked out of his trance by a ringing phone. He looked at the screen and saw it was Detective Hanks. "Cindy, have you found something?"

"How is she?"

He glanced toward the beautiful woman on the bed. Her face was pale, the lush lips quivering under a dream and the damp curtain of mahogany hair was spread over her pillow in a silky fan. "She's tired but otherwise good."

"Good. Your boy is worried about her. He's been whining at the door since he arrived."

Matthew started for the door. "I'll come get him. Thank Tremwell for delivering him to the station will you? In case I miss him."

"Sure. I don't think he minded. In fact I had to wrench the little guy out of his arms."

Matthew punched the elevator button and stood to the side as a man with long, gray hair and a diamond stud in one ear stepped out, thanking him in a Middle Eastern accent. Matthew nodded and moved past into the elevator. "Max has really taken a liking to Alex. He was growling at the ambulance attendants when they tried to tend to her."

"I don't think he's the only one who's taken a liking to Miss Alex."

Matthew frowned. He hadn't thought he was that obvious. "I'm just concerned about her safety. After what happened to Cam…"

"Yeah, it's a bit unnerving. But if he wanted her dead he would have used real bullets."

"Right." Matthew frowned. "So he apparently doesn't want her dead."

"So why target her for attacks?" Hanks asked. "Not once but twice."

"I have no clue. But I intend to find out. I'm on my way to the station now. Did you assign someone to guard Alex?"

"I did. Officer Blount should be there very shortly. You might pass her on the way out."

The elevator doors slid open and Matthew found himself facing a young female officer with an intense blue gaze. "Here she is. I'll talk to you later, Hanks." Matthew extended his hand and introduced himself, quickly filling the officer in on their situation. "I need you to make sure she's safe while she's here. Nobody goes in except her doctor and nurses. Stop at the nurse's station as soon as you get to the floor and make them introduce you to everybody who needs to go into Alex's room."

Blount nodded. "Yes, sir." She stepped past him and entered the elevator. Matthew stood in the hallway for a moment, reluctant to leave Alex alone in the hospital. Something was bothering him and he couldn't put his finger on it. But with nothing substantial to keep him there, Matthew figured his time would be better spent trying to find the killer before he found Alex again.

And finished the job he'd started.

~SC~

She looked so peaceful lying there. Such a pretty woman. She'd be a wonderful addition to his portfolio of kills. And so intelligent. In fact, her intelligence had been the only thing that saved her after he killed her predecessor. His instincts had been to remove all obstacles to finding what he wanted. But he quickly realized, when assessing the opposition as he always did, that if anyone could find that flash drive, it would be her. So he let her live for a while. And he'd been right. She was getting close.

Too close.

It was probably time to reel her in and add her to his collection.

The thought made his palms itch. He couldn't wait to introduce her to her own personal Hell. In fact he was busily crafting it in his mind at that very moment.

"Sir?"

He turned and smiled. The cop was young and attractive. She had pretty blue eyes, her gaze sharp. "Hello."

"Is there something I can help you with?"

He shook his head. "I'm sorry. I was just passing by after visiting my mother down the hall. I thought I knew this woman but I realize she's not the person I thought she was."

The cop's searching gaze slid toward the bed. "In that case, I'm afraid I'll have to ask you to leave. She isn't taking any visitors right now."

The woman on the bed stirred, her eyes opening. She blinked a few times, looking confused as she found him standing there. Then her gaze widened and he smiled. "Of course. I'm very sorry." He turned his smile on the young cop. "You have a nice day."

"Thank you, sir. You too."

His step was light as he left. The games were afoot. And he couldn't wait to play.

~SC~

Alex frowned at the petite cop by the door. "Who are you? And who was that man?"

The cop fixed a worried gaze on her. "Officer Tammy Blount. I'm your protection for the day. He…" She stepped into the hall and looked in the direction the man had gone. "I'm not sure who he was."

Alex didn't like the lines of worry between the cop's brows. "Maybe you should find out."

Officer Blount nodded. "I'm just going to the nurse's station. I'll keep an eye on your door."

Alex elevated the head of her bed. "Go. I'm fine." She scanned the room for her cell phone and then realized with disgust that it would be ruined. It had been in her pocket when she fell into the canal. The thought made her skin itch. She really needed to get a shower. There was no telling what disgusting organisms were brewing in that water.

She pressed the call button and was relieved when a heavyset woman in scrubs came into her room, her wide face pleasantly serious. "Are you all right, hun?"

"I need a phone, can you get me one?"

"Certainly. I'll be right back."

Alex shoved back her covers and swung her legs over the side of the bed. A wave of dizziness swamped her but she pushed through it and stood. She went to the closet and grimaced when she realized there wouldn't be any clothing there. Her clothes were no doubt drenched and slimed.

The nurse returned and blinked when she saw Alex out of bed. "Oh no, hun. You shouldn't be on your feet yet."

Alex glanced at the woman's name badge. "I'm fine. Really, Marta is it? I need to talk to Detective Cindy Hanks from the IMPD. It's vitally important."

The nurse plugged in the phone she'd carried into the room. "We don't get too many requests for land lines anymore." She grinned. "Most people have their cell phones nowadays."

Alex sat down on the bed, barely suppressing a groan of relief, and reached for the phone. "Do you think I could borrow a set of scrubs? I need to get out of here."

The nurse shook her head. "You need to be released by the doctor…"

"I'm leaving either way. I don't need the doctor's permission. But I'm begging you not to make me climb into a taxi with my behind exposed to God and everybody."

The nurse sighed. "I'll find you something."

"Thank you." Alex quickly dialed Detective Hanks' number.

The detective answered after three rings. "Hanks."

"This is Alex McFadden. I wondered if you'd come up with any recent victims using my information."

"Alex. Aren't you in the hospital?"

"Not for long. Please answer my question."

"I sent three possibles to your inbox. You were right. The ME reports on all of them listed at least three resuscitations for each victim."

Alex grimaced. "I would have liked to have been wrong about that one."

"I know. This killer is truly evil. It appears that Cam was just his most recent victim."

"Were you able to isolate how he picks his victims?" Alex asked. Nurse Marta came into the room with a set of scrubs bearing puppies and kittens and some slippers wrapped in cellophane. She mouthed "thank you" to the woman and started tugging on the ties holding her gown together.

"No. That's the biggest sticking point and the reason he most likely has gotten away with killing for a decade or more. The victims are different ages, sexes and socio-economic backgrounds. One was hung from a light fixture. One was strangled in bed with a favorite scarf. One was drowned in her own bathtub."

Alex tucked the phone between her ear and shoulder. "I think I might know where the information is that Cam has on the killer. I'm going to the office to get it. Do you want to meet me there?"

"Absolutely. Shall I pick you up at the hospital?"

"No. But you have an officer here. Maybe you can tell her to drive me to Smart Investigations?"

"Sure. Put officer Blount on the phone and I'll tell her."

Alex looked up as footsteps sounded beyond her door. It was a woman with two young children. She smiled when she saw Alex looking at her and kept on walking, her hands full with two rambunctious toddlers. "I'll tell her when she gets back."

"Back? Her orders were to stay on that door. Where did she go?"

"Just down the hall a ways to the nurse's station. She

has eyes on the door."

"Okay." Hanks didn't sound happy. "Make sure she calls me right away when she gets back. Oh, and Alex, I ran that tattoo you drew through our database and didn't come up with anything."

"What does that mean?"

"Maybe nothing. The ink could be new. Or the guy wearing it just might have managed to stay out of the system. But it was a good thought."

Alex hung up, frustrated by another dead end and feeling badly for probably getting Officer Blount into trouble with her boss. But she couldn't worry about those things at the moment. The solution to the missing flash drive had come to her as she slept. She was pretty sure she knew where Cam had hidden it. And he'd left clues to its whereabouts all over the place. She just hadn't been sharp enough to recognize them. On the heels of that thought was the realization that Cam must have known he was in danger. He'd trusted Matthew enough to leave subtle clues only he could follow. It was only a matter of time before Matthew figured it out. If he hadn't already done it. But the most important thing in that moment was to get the evidence into the hands of the police so they could mobilize to catch the killer before he killed again.

When she was dressed, Alex went out into the hallway looking for Officer Blount. The cop was nowhere to be seen. Alex headed for the nurse's station. Seeing Nurse Marta, she approached and asked, "Do you know where Officer Blount went?"

The nurse looked up, her eyes widening. "I thought she headed back to your room." The woman frowned. "Maybe she went to the ladies instead."

Alex's gaze followed Nurse Marta's to the restroom doors across from the elevator. "That must be it. I'll look for her there." She started away and stopped, turning back. "Did you know anything about the man she was talking to?"

The nurse frowned. "No. Like I told that young officer, I've never seen him before. And we don't have any patients matching the description he gave the officer on this floor."

Alex's pulse sped and panic slipped down her spine. She started toward the end of the hallway and the stairs. "Call the police. Detective Hanks. Tell her he was here and her cop is missing." When Nurse Marta frowned, Alex shook her head. "She'll understand. I've got to go."

# CHAPTER FIFTEEN

Matthew stepped aside to let two twenty-something women exit from the station. He thought he recognized them from the cafeteria. They were chatting animatedly, nibbling on snacks. Matthew's gaze found the chocolate bar clutched in the taller woman's hand and he watched as she lifted it to her mouth, taking a dainty bite. The action sent a jolt through his system as Matthew suddenly realized where Cam had hidden the flash drive. He realized something else as well. Pulling out his phone, Matthew quickly dialed a number he'd recently called. It rang three times before a woman answered. "Hello?"

"Mrs. Snow, this is Matthew Smart."

"Hello, Mr. Smart…"

"I'm sorry, ma'am, but I need to know, have you spoken to your ex-husband since we saw you last?"

"Why no, I…"

"Can you call him? Find out where he is?"

When she hesitated he added, "It's very important, Mrs. Snow. I promise I wouldn't ask you to do it if it wasn't important. It's a matter of life or death."

He thought he heard the sifting of breath over the phone. She was obviously not thrilled at the prospect of calling her ex.

"Okay. I'll call you back at this number?"

"Yes. As soon as possible. Thank you."

Matthew disconnected and ran into the precinct, heading toward the elevators that would take him to Hanks' office. The Information Officer stopped him before he climbed onto the elevator. "Mr. Smart? If you're looking for Hanks she's not here."

"Where is she?"

"She got a call from some woman at St. Joseph's Hospital and she bolted out of here with a contingent of squad cars."

Panic climbed Matthew's throat. "Was it Alex McFadden?"

The officer frowned. "Sir?"

"The woman who called her. Was her name Alex?"

"She didn't say. She told me to give you a message though." The man handed Matthew a piece of note paper, folded in half. He opened it to find a couple of quickly scrawled sentences. Alex is in danger. She's left the hospital. I think she might be going to the office.

Matthew swore and took off running. At the door he remembered Max. He turned back. "My dog…"

"Tremwell has him. Detective Hanks said to tell you he'd be fine until you got back."

Matthew nodded and exploded out the door. With traffic he was a half hour from the office. He prayed Alex would be all right until he got there.

He had a really bad feeling about the way things were going down.

~SC~

Alex locked the office door behind her and leaned against it, taking several deep breaths to calm her wildly beating heart. Fighting a feeling of terror that she was being stalked, she forced her feet to move quickly toward Matthew's office. The phone rang as she approached his desk and, without thinking, Alex answered it. "Smart Investigations." A brief silence sent Alex's pulse spiking. She was suddenly certain she'd announced her location to a killer.

"Ms. McFadden?"

She didn't recognize the voice but thought she should. "Who's calling please?"

"I'm sorry. This is Professor Deets. At IUPUI?"

Relief spun through her and she dropped into Matthew's chair. Of course. The slight accent. "Yes. This is Alex. How can I help you, Professor?"

"Mr. Smart told me to call if I remembered something."

"Yes. Did you?" She sat forward, sliding her fingers through the candy dish with the mint flavored chocolates. Her fingertips struck something anchored to the glass. Alex pulled the bowl closer and dumped its contents. One mint stayed attached to the bottom.

"I remembered a phone call Cameron and I had about a week before his death. He asked me about a serial killer called The Collector."

The candy was taped to the glass bottom with transparent shipping tape. She started to pry the mint away from the bottom but her fingers stilled at the professor's words. "I remember that case. The police arrested the killer in the home of his last victim."

"Yes. That's what they believed. But the case was sketchy at best. The man they arrested had been detained before for burglary and he claimed the woman was already dead when he entered the home. However, after he was incarcerated, there were no more murders that fit his mode of killing."

Alex sat back in the chair, her attention fully caught. "It doesn't sound like you believe he was The Collector?"

"I did. Until Cameron brought him up to me. Then I started to wonder. What if the man they arrested was the wrong guy? What if the real killer changed his method just enough to fool the police?"

"That would be difficult for him to do, right? This type of killer relies heavily on a particular and precise method because it represents the genesis of their killing spree."

"Yes. It would be difficult. But we're dealing with a man who 'collects' the best of every skill. His kills represent the most talented singer, the most skilled pianist, the most celebrated author, business mogul, and politician. He would perceive himself to be the best at what he does too. And built into that would be his ability to adjust when necessary to stay ahead of the police."

"That makes a horrifying kind of sense," she agreed. "You think that's what Cam was chasing? What he might have been killed for discovering?"

"I don't know, Ms. McFadden. But it seems very possible."

The papers on Matthew's desk fluttered and her head came up. "Thank you, Professor," she said softly before hanging up. Someone had opened the outer door and closed it softly enough that she hadn't heard.

The killer was there.

Alex reached for the candy bowl with shaking fingers. She didn't have much time.

~SC~

Matthew smacked the horn on his car as the light changed. The cars on the busy streets apparently had drivers with molasses for blood. It took them a good ten seconds to even start moving after the light changed. He'd missed two lights because the cars in front of him seemed to think they had all the time in the world.

His cell rang and he answered it almost before it stopped ringing the first time. "Smart."

"Mr. Smart, it's Leanne Snow."

The woman sounded upset, her voice tense. "What is it, Mrs. Snow? What's wrong?"

"I don't know. I'm confused. I just spoke to my

husband and he lied to me."

Matthew hit the brakes as the light ahead turned yellow and the three cars in front of him screeched to a halt. He swore softly. "I'm really short on time, Mrs. Snow. Can you explain very quickly?"

"He claims he's still on the road. He left this morning so he'd make it in time for Roberta's funeral."

Matthew's hands tightened on the wheel. "Your husband isn't in Indy?"

"He has to be, doesn't he? You spoke to him yourself."

Matthew barely resisted throwing his phone. Instead he disconnected and hit the gas, threading the SUV into a space too small for it and running two tires up over the curb as he gunned it toward the intersection ahead. He swung the big car into the turn just ahead of a pickup truck speeding through the intersection with the green light.

He gunned it as the truck squealed to a stop, its driver pounding the horn in anger. Matthew barely noticed. He'd been played by a killer and he'd never seen it coming. But to make things worse, he wasn't the one who would pay the price. It was Alex who, for whatever reason, was caught in the killer's crosshairs. And Matthew, in his arrogance and stupidity, had let it happen.

~SC~

Alex peered through the crack between the door and the frame. The man from the hospital, the one who'd been staring at her when she woke up, was standing just inside the door. He had a secretive little smile on his face and his gaze was fixed on the room directly across from the entrance.

The room where they'd found Cam's body.

Ice prickled along her spine and her breathing quickened. The dark orbs of the man's gaze were bereft of feeling. Only the curve of his lips gave any indication of his mood.

Alex had no doubt she was looking at Cam's killer. A

man who killed not only without regret…but also with pleasure. Gregg Pence's words slithered through her mind, making her shudder.

He had dead eyes. Cold and cruel.

The killer's gaze suddenly turned in her direction, locking on the door as if he could see her behind it. Alex swallowed a cry of alarm and stepped quickly backwards. Her gaze flashed around the room, looking for a weapon. Any weapon.

She'd give anything in that moment for her gun. But it was probably with Matthew. Along with her purse. He wouldn't have left it at the hospital when she was unconscious. It was a good thing Alex knew where Matthew kept the spare office key. But she'd locked the door behind her. Or had she? Her mind wasn't working as efficiently as usual. Probably because of the headache raging behind her eyes.

Footsteps sounded on the other side of the door and Alex panicked.

He was coming for her.

She hurried across the room and started pulling open drawers, looking for a spare weapon. She found a knife in the bottom drawer, nestled between the front of the drawer and a dense stack of manila folders. She grabbed it, clutching it tightly in her hand just as the door swung open with a prolonged creak.

"Hello again, Ms. McFadden."

Alex's head came up and she dropped into Matthew's chair. Her gaze rose and she did her best to force a neutral expression onto her face. "We haven't formally met. But I'm guessing that you're The Collector?" She clutched the knife in her hand, hiding the blade behind her arm as her fingers tightened around its leather-wrapped hilt.

The man's eyes widened slightly and his smile widened. "Very good, Alex." He tilted his head. "You don't mind if I call you Alex, do you?"

Something about the man's voice was familiar but her

mind was racing and she couldn't lock down where she'd heard it before. "Sure. If you tell me your name so I know what to call you."

"You already know my name." He leaned against the doorframe, to all appearances totally relaxed.

"I know the name the police gave you. But that isn't your name, is it?" Alex prayed Detective Hanks would arrive in time to save her. But if she didn't, Alex didn't plan to go down without a fight. She shifted in the chair and barely stopped herself from gasping as the tip of the knife pierced her flesh.

At least she knew it was sharp.

The killer nodded. "It's true, The Collector wouldn't have been the name I'd have given myself. It lacks a certain…"

"Menace?" Alex wrapped her toes around the base of the chair and flicked her gaze quickly around the space. If she was really fast…

He chuckled darkly. "That works." He pushed away from the door and started toward her. "But enough about me. Let's spend some time getting to know you. I'm afraid we don't have as much time as I'd like." He stopped on the other side of Matthew's desk and lifted a brow. "I'd like to spend days on you, watching your fiery will drain away a drop at a time." Before she could figure out what he had in mind, he grasped the edge of the desk and shoved it into her.

With a scream of pure agony, she dropped the knife and it hit the plastic floor protector beneath the chair. Pain sheared through Alex's ribs and the chair skated backward, slamming against the wall as he leapt the desk and landed next to her, his hands pinning her arms to the armrests.

"Whatever you were scheming, lovely Alex, I'm afraid it just isn't going to work out as planned."

She tried to kick out but he trapped her legs against the chair with his thighs. His hot breath fanned across her face and his lips descended, touching her mouth so lightly she thought she'd imagined it as he whipped his head back to avoid her head butt.

He laughed. "I knew you were going to be a challenge. I'm pleased to realize I was right."

"The police are on their way."

He laughed again. "I'm afraid they're very busy dealing with poor Officer Blount." He shook his head. "It's such a shame when someone so young and fresh dies, isn't it, Alex?"

Alex closed her eyes as her stomach twisted with regret and fear. That poor woman was only trying to protect Alex. And she was killed by a madman for her efforts. She opened her eyes and stared into his face, not wanting to give him even a second's pleasure from her pain. "You're a monster."

He shrugged. "Maybe. Or maybe I'm just a superior being who loves the finer things in life." He leaned close again and pressed his forehead against hers, forcing it against the back of the chair before she could try to slam it into him again. Alex struggled but he was just too strong. "Emotions are such messy things, Alex. They cause people to make stupid mistakes. They create much more pain in the long run than rational thought ever could."

He bit her lip hard enough to make it bleed and Alex squealed before she could stop herself. Then he lifted his head and pressed something against her chest, between her breasts.

Fire exploded through her torso and her limbs stiffened, sheering skin off her shins as they connected against the underside of the desk. Her body twitched manically, her head slamming against the chair. And all thought of escape was lost.

# CHAPTER SIXTEEN

Matthew slammed the office door open, his gun clutched two handed before him. He knew he'd lost the advantage of surprise with the move, but he was desperate to interrupt the killer in his deadly work before he could do to Alex what he'd done to Cam. The thought created a giant, icy knot in his gut that nearly brought him to his knees. He had to be in time. The alternative was just unfathomable.

Matthew moved quickly away from the door, toward the open stock room door. Déjà vu slammed over him, making stars of panic burst before his eyes. The light was on in the long, narrow room. Matthew stilled just outside the room, his gun ready, and listened hard for any sound that might give him an idea what he would find when he stepped through the door.

Silence beat against him, turning his gut to lead as his imagination forged a picture of Alex, sitting still and lifeless like a porcelain doll in the swivel chair from behind her desk.

His gaze shot toward her desk and he felt a moment's relief as he saw her chair.

The relief didn't last long though. There was no reason

to believe the man would follow the same pattern he'd followed with Cam. If he'd brought her to the supply room, it would have been simply to send Matthew a message. He'd won another contest. He continued to be the best at what he did. He was a king among killers. And Matthew had been found wanting.

A bead of sweat slipped down his brow and stung his eye as panic turned to a rotating blade inside his gut and ripped him wide open at the realization. He had failed. He had been found wanting. And beautiful Alex would end up paying the price.

Matthew swallowed down the raging fear of what he would find and ducked through the door, his gun up and his finger on the trigger. His heart pounded so loudly he feared the killer would hear him coming. Her name trembled on his lips. His heart already heavy with the certainty of what he would find. And when he saw the chair...the rope hanging from the fixture high above...Matthew's legs gave out from underneath him and he had to catch himself against the door frame to keep from falling.

~SC~

She came awake with a start, jerking against the restraints holding her to the gurney. Fear clamped an icy hand over her heart and squeezed, making dots ping before her gaze. She tried to swallow but realized her throat was constricted. Not completely...just enough to make it hard to breathe and nearly impossible to swallow.

Alex's gaze flashed around the room, taking in the damp walls and the dim light. A single, bare bulb hung above her head, dancing softly on an errant wisp of air. She tried to lift her head and the rope cut into her skin, choking her as it pressed against her throat.

Her chest heaving on a cough she couldn't complete, Alex fought the debilitating pull of panic, shoving it brutally aside so she could think.

How had she gotten there? The last thing she remembered was the killer jabbing her with something that burned like fire. Taser. As she had the thought the spot between her breasts burned in remembered pain and her head throbbed to the beat of her racing heart.

Alex pushed it all away. She was an intelligent woman. She could find her way out of her current mess. She had to. Nobody knew where she was. Nobody would be coming to help her. There was only her.

Her and a madman.

What did she know about the killer? The Collector. The report she'd pulled together for Detective Hanks had outlined the potential suspect. Older male, most likely alone in the world, had domineering parents or a single parent who constantly berated him for failing to live up to their standards. So when he'd gotten old enough, he'd created his own standards and then his own methods of killing. Alex figured The Collector had probably killed his parents or parent as a teen. Since he used various methods of asphyxiation she assumed that was how he'd done it. And though he'd mixed it up a bit over the years…his method of killing hadn't changed. Only the tools he used to deprive his victims of air had changed.

So he planned to asphyxiate her. Alex carefully lifted her head just enough to look at the rest of her body. A thick rope bound her wrist and snaked underneath the gurney, connecting it to the other wrist. He'd bound her legs the same way. She tried to tug against them to see if there was any play in the rope. Her eyes widened. She couldn't lift her arms or legs. She was paralyzed!

Panic swirled through her chest again and she thought she would pass out. The world swam around her in charcoal shapes. But Alex closed her eyes and forced herself to breathe…to think.

It was very unlikely she was actually paralyzed. He'd probably just given her something that would simulate paralysis. She concentrated hard on her hands and, sure enough, she felt a very slight tingling.

The drug was starting to wear off.

Her relief from that realization was short lived. She'd need to wait out the effects of the mystery drug before she could even begin to try to get free. And since she couldn't lift her head enough to see her body, and she couldn't feel it either, she was completely helpless for an unknown length of time. Frustration brought tears to her eyes. Alex blinked them angrily away. There had to be a way out of the trap the killer had set for her. But to figure it out, she first had to determine how the trap was built.

So she set her mind to that.

~SC~

Matthew scrubbed a hand over his face and forced himself to move closer to the chair, which he recognized as his office chair. There was blood on the metal frame of the armrest, but it was the thing hanging from the end of the rope that really made his blood turn cold. He reached out and touched the thick ribbon of silky, mahogany colored hair. "Oh God, Alex…" It was clearly a message to him. And Matthew was obviously too late.

He stepped away from the scene, clenching his hand into a fist as the sensory memory of her silky hair burned against his skin. He wasn't too late. He couldn't be. Matthew would find Alex and kill the man responsible for hurting her.

He turned away and hurried to his office, noting the dislocated desk and finding more blood on the floor beneath where the chair had been. On his desk was a piece of paper with a single sentence typed on its surface.

Bring me the stick or she dies.

Matthew reached toward the page, his finger hovering above it. He resisted the urge to rip it into hundreds of little pieces and send it to the floor. He needed to remain calm if he was to find her. He needed to use what he knew…the tools he had available to him.

Matthew considered calling Hanks but it wasn't time. First he had to find her and kill the sonofabitch who'd hurt her.

Then he'd call the police.

Matthew pulled the keyboard drawer out and started typing. A moment later the security feed for his outside cameras came on. He quickly rewound the camera for the back of the building, the one that was visible to anyone who bothered to look, high on the corner of his building. That tape showed the alleyway with a couple of cars and a plain white van parked alongside the building and then suddenly nothing. The killer had dispatched it.

"Let's see if you're as good as you think you are." Matthew brought up the feed for the second, hidden security camera. The one he'd nestled inside a lush green box shrub at the edge of the property. A moment later he had a visual on the killer. Something about the guy was familiar, like he'd come face to face with him at some point. But he couldn't place exactly where.

The guy disappeared inside the building and Matthew fast forwarded several minutes...past the trash truck that came to empty the dumpster and a couple of skate boarders using the alley as a track.

Finally, he saw what he was looking for. The man came back outside, pulling a large trash can with a lid behind him. He proceeded to pull the can toward the nondescript white van and loaded it onto a lift, shoving it inside and closing the back doors. As he pulled away, Matthew jotted down the license plate number. "Gotcha." He quickly dialed a friend at BMV.

"Bureau of Motor Vehicles, this is Tiffany."

"Hey, Tiff. It's Matthew. Can you run down a license number for me?" Matthew recited the letters and numbers he'd written down.

"Sure. Just give me a minute."

Matthew stared out the window behind his desk as he waited. He already had an idea where the killer had to be holed up. It was too much of a coincidence that he happened to be down at the canal at the exact same time he and Alex were there earlier in the day. Either the guy was following the police, scoping out their investigation, or…"

"It's stolen, Matthew. If you've found it you should tell the cops."

He frowned. "Where was it stolen from, Tiff?"

"The Ornate Duck. It's an art gallery down by the canal. My sister lives in one of the condos down there and she and I visited the gallery once. It was a nice place."

"Was?"

"Yeah. I don't think they're in business anymore, but I remember seeing a fleet of those plain white vans parked behind their building."

Matthew thanked her and disconnected. He turned to the candy dish sitting at the very edge of the desk, just about ready to fall over. If the killer had shoved the desk one more time he'd have probably found what he was looking for. Matthew dumped the candy and tugged the taped chocolate off the bottom, scooping up the flash drive.

A moment later he was running down the steps and out the door. He estimated that, barring heavy traffic, his destination was twenty tense minutes away. He wouldn't have the element of surprise on his side. But he'd have something a lot more useful. He was pissed off and more than a little desperate. The killer would have a better shot dealing with a rabid buffalo.

# CHAPTER SEVENTEEN

Blood slicked the ropes holding her arms and legs to the gurney. The rope around her throat had tightened as she threw herself from side to side in an effort to loosen it. The tightening caused her to panic and fight harder as she realized the pressure on her throat only went one way.

It constricted, but it didn't release.

A soft sob of terror escaped Alex's lips as she realized she was going to die. Her struggles had brought her nothing but closer to that unthinkable outcome. Her gaze slid to the camera blinking high in the corner of the basement room. She'd quickly realized he had to be watching her and, for a while, she stopped struggling because she didn't want to give him the satisfaction. Whatever drug he'd given her to numb her limbs was slowly wearing off and she could feel the rough scrape of her restraints against her skin and the pain that rubbing left behind.

Alex's mind still worked, trying to find a way out of her current predicament. As near as she could tell, the rope around her throat wasn't tied or knotted behind her head. It seemed to be strung to either side and attached to something on the concrete block wall. If she could just figure out how to push the gurney toward the wall…

The door opened across the room and Alex stilled. A man she didn't recognize slipped through the opening, a cold light in his eyes. "Well, well. It looks like you've gotten yourself in quite a pickle, Alex." Though the man's longish dark hair and pasty complexion weren't familiar, Alex had definitely heard the voice before. Or some mutation of the voice. She was starting to realize The Collector had many faces and personalities. And he was a master at switching between them. The man she watched stride toward her was smaller in frame than the man she'd met before. He looked shorter and less padded. But the gait was similar. There was a certain smug cockiness in the way he walked. She'd noted that smugness before.

The killer stopped at the end of the gurney and placed his hands on her feet. She tried to wrench away from his touch but the ropes held her firm.

"Let me go."

"I'm afraid I can't do that, dear."

She decided her best bet was to keep him talking. In case someone was coming for her. "You knew I was in the office."

"I followed you there."

"Why did you tell me so much? About yourself and the arrest?"

He shrugged. "You won't live to tell anyone. Besides, it's fun to share my notoriety. It was very annoying when the police arrested the wrong man. That bumbling idiot could never have done what I've done."

"What have you done? You've killed a bunch of people who didn't deserve to die. The books are filled with murderous thugs who've done the same. You're not special. You're just sick."

He clenched his jaw, the hands covering her feet tightening painfully against her skin. But after a moment he seemed to calm. "I've been watching you, Alex." He shook his head, frowning. "I'll admit I'm a bit disappointed. I'd thought with all your brain power you'd have come up with something by now." He shook his head and smiled. "If you're not going to entertain me with your inventiveness, I guess there's no point in keeping you alive." His hands tightened on her feet and he pulled the gurney toward him, cutting off the small amount of air she could still draw. The rope compressed her airways, sending her pulse skyward as her eyes bulged and she flailed helplessly. Bright spots of color burst before her eyes as the rope cut into her windpipe, agony blooming beneath an uncompromising terror.

Her lips opened on a scream she couldn't accomplish and tears slipped down her cheeks as oxygen deprivation turned her body dull. A moment later the light started to slip away and the terrified beat of her heart slowed. Alex's mind rebelled in one last burst of rage as death pulled her close, and wrapped her body in smothering arms.

~SC~

Alex swam back to consciousness on a desperate gasp for air. She opened her eyes and swallowed painfully, jerking in surprise as his hated face appeared above her.

He chuckled. "That was fun. Tell me, Alex, is it true what they say about a bright light and all that? I've always wondered." He reached out and scraped a finger over her cheek, harvesting a tear she hadn't known escaped.

"Go to Hell." The words barely scraped past her raw throat. They came out rusty and fractured. But the killer standing over her heard them just the same.

He lifted midnight eyebrows that looked like they'd been shaped with tweezers. "Such hostility. I'd have expected you to take this as a challenge, my dear. Instead you're just another victim." Shaking his head, he patted her hand. "Such a shame."

Alex acted on pure instinct. She whipped her hand around and grasped his, digging her nails into his pale flesh with a desperate kind of strength.

He cried out, clearly surprised, and stepped away from the gurney as she threw herself against the restraints with a feral scream.

The door across the room slammed open and Matthew came through, his gun held in two hands. He fired at the killer and the man dove behind the gurney, throwing himself against it from behind. Alex made a gurgling sound as the rope ravaged her throat again and she grappled for a breath. The killer tugged harder, until she feared the rope would cut her airways in half.

Matthew stilled, clearly afraid to fire for fear of hitting Alex. "Stop!" He lifted his hands in the air, the gun pointed toward the ceiling.

"Put down the gun and throw the flash drive over here."

Matthew did as he was told, his gaze locked on Alex. He set the gun on the floor and kicked it away, then threw the flash drive he'd retrieved from the office across the floor. It skittered under the gurney and was stopped by a large foot.

Alex jerked her right hand free and reached up to grasp the rope around her throat. She wrapped her fingers around it, channeling her desperation into a final attempt to relieve pressure on her throat. The gurney slammed backward, hitting the concrete block wall behind her.

The killer put the gurney between him and Matthew and ran, diving through the room's only exit as Matthew grabbed his discarded gun and fired again.

As soon as the killer disappeared through the door, Matthew hurried over to help Alex. His hands worked the ropes tying her to the gurney, skimming reassuringly over her limbs as he pulled her free. "Alex. Thank God you're alive."

Alex coughed violently, tugging on the remaining restraints. "Get these…" She succumbed to violent coughing and couldn't finish.

"I've got them, just hold on, honey."

When she was free, Alex tried to jump from the gurney. Matthew grabbed her arm. "Hold on, Alex. You need to take a breath."

She shook her head. "He's getting away," she croaked. "We need to…" Coughing overtook her again.

Matthew pointed toward the floor behind the gurney. "He won't get away. Look. He's wounded."

She followed where he was pointing and, sure enough, there was a trail of bright droplets, leading toward the door. She nodded, grabbing Matthew's hand. "Let's go get him."

Matthew opened his mouth to respond just as gunshots sounded above, followed by shouts and more gunshots. "The cavalry's here. He's not getting away."

She didn't care. Alex was glad Matthew had brought the police but she was going to kill the sonofabitch herself. She stumbled toward the door and found herself facing a steep set of wooden steps. Her throat burning and her legs prickling painfully as blood rushed back into them, Alex grabbed the railing and started up. Matthew came up behind her and wrapped an arm around her waist, all but hauling her up the steps with his gun held in front of them.

They emerged from the stairwell and stopped. Matthew let go of her waist and leaned close to speak softly into her ear. "The police are outside. He's going to be desperate. Don't get too close."

She nodded and stepped out. "You're trapped," she told the killer. "You're either dealing with them or us."

The killer whipped around, one arm hanging limp and bloody at his side. He held a large box knife in one hand and leaned against the door, breathing heavily. "You won't kill me."

Matthew and Alex shared a look. Then Matthew lifted the gun, jerking it toward the back of the large showroom.

Through the glass Alex could see the flashing lights of the police cars and hear someone yelling through a bull horn.

"Move away from the windows," Matthew told the man.

The killer's eyes were wild, his hair matted and bloody on one side He looked from the windows to Matthew, seemingly trying to decide which option was less suicidal.

Matthew focused his gun on the kill zone in the center of the man's broad chest. "This is over, Professor Deets. We have everything we need to put you in prison."

The professor smiled. "Are you sure?" He looked down at a plastic dish on the floor at his feet and kicked it toward Matthew and Alex. Cam's flash drive was floating in the dish, immersed in liquid that smelled like paint thinner. "I believe real evidence is going to be harder to come by than you think."

Alex clenched her fists and started toward him.

"Alex!" Matthew's voice was filled with panic.

Deets lifted the knife and smiled. "Come and get me, dear. If I'm going down at least I'll have your lovely blood on my hands."

"Alex! Stop."

She dragged herself to a stop and stood there, her hands fisted. "I want to hit him."

A SWAT team glided past the windows at the killer's back. It was only a matter of time before they took their shot. They were probably trying to assess the danger to Matthew and Alex. Matthew's hand wrapped around her wrist, pulling her toward the stairwell wall.

As he pulled her back, Matthew spoke to Deets, no doubt trying to distract him. "You've had a nice long run, Deets. If that's your real name."

Deets shrugged, then grimaced as the action flexed his shoulder wound. "I am a man of many names and faces."

"Yes," Matthew said thoughtfully. "You mentioned you taught theatre. I should have put the pieces together. "I'll admit your disguises were damn good."

The man lifted his uninjured arm and bowed. "I believe

in excelling at all things."

"Like killing people?" Alex asked, her lip curling with disgust.

He smiled. "My dear. I don't kill them. I enshrine them. Make them immortal. Their deaths, excruciating and unique, are like the final bow before the curtain drops. My victims are carefully chosen for their specialness." His expression turned warm and he skimmed a gaze over Alex. "Just as you were."

Cindy Hanks' voice came through the bull horn. "Come on out, Professor Deets. It's over."

Deets threw the windows an anxious look. He must have seen SWAT because he stepped away from the glass, moving nearer Matthew and Alex. "Surely you can understand what I have to offer the world. It's a complex and competitive place, the realm we live in. The special ones deserve to be lifted out of the muck, elevated from the swarms of cattle they're surrounded by. They thank me for helping them rise. I see it in their eyes as they breathe their last breath."

Alex turned to Matthew. "The police are going to kill him. He doesn't deserve a quick death." She saw the moment Matthew realized she was right. The bullhorn had gone silent. SWAT had to be in place. "We don't have much time," she said.

Matthew looked into her eyes, no doubt reading her intent there. She could only hope he respected her for her strength rather than fearing the intensity of hate he no doubt saw. "Are you sure?"

"Never more sure."

Matthew nodded. "Okay then."

The killer's gaze slid to Matthew and held, fear obvious in the faded blue eyes. He slowly lifted his hands, dropping the knife. "Okay. I surrender. You don't need to shoot me."

"He's right. We don't need to shoot him," Matthew told Alex.

Alex's jaw tightened as rage suffused her. "No. We don't."

Matthew lifted his gun, pointing it at the killer. He caught Alex's gaze. "It's gonna kill me to step back from this but..." He smiled at the man cowering against the wall. "He's all yours."

Alex expelled a long breath, ignoring the fiery pain in her throat, and inclined her chin. Then she started to run, leaping off the ground a few feet away from Deets and brutally kicking him on the side of the head. He went down hard, his skull bouncing against the tile floor before his eyes rolled back and he went out cold. "That's for all the people you've tortured and killed, asswipe."

"I didn't know you could do that," Matthew said with grim respect. "I thought you might give him a little girly punch in the gut or something."

Alex snorted. "There's a lot you don't know about me, Smart."

He moved close, wrapping an arm around her waist and pulling her close. "And I'm really looking forward to learning it all," he told her. Then he pulled her into a kiss that curled her toes and sent the horror in that basement room spinning away. Leaving behind only heated thoughts and delicious sensations that she couldn't wait to explore.

# CHAPTER EIGHTEEN

"Have you spoken to Alex since the arrest?"

Matthew's fingers ruffled the soft fur between Max's shoulders. "No. I told her to take a couple of days off. I figured I'd leave her alone while she decided if she wanted to keep her job."

Hanks laughed. "It was a hell of a first week."

Matthew pulled to the curb and stopped the car, gazing at the building across the street. "Yeah. It certainly was. That was my fault. I shouldn't have hired anybody until I found out why Cam was killed."

"It doesn't sound to me like she gave you much choice." In the hours after Deets' arrest, Hanks and Matthew had had a lot of time to kill. They'd sat together in the emergency room at the hospital while Alex's injuries were tended and Officer Blount was stitched back together. The young officer had been found at the bottom of a stairwell at the hospital, with several broken bones and a nasty concussion. But she would live. Thank God. Deets had been responsible for way too many deaths as it was.

While they'd sat together, Matthew had shared with Cindy why he'd hired Alex and had even hinted at his feelings for her. He'd told Hanks why he didn't think he could, or should, hire Alex on a permanent basis. The cop hadn't said much but Matthew got the impression she agreed. Workplace romances were never a good idea. They tended to demean everyone involved.

"I hired her because I thought she was smart and intuitive and she is all that. Plus she works harder than anybody I know. It's just not right that she's going to be punished because I'm thinking with the wrong body part."

"Sounds to me like you're thinking with the right part. You just have to put the kibosh on the other stuff. If anybody deserves that job it's Alex."

A light came on behind the window he was watching and a tall, shapely form glided past, the sheer curtains transforming her into a decadent shadow. "Assuming she still wants it," Matthew said. The shadow passed in front of the window again and halted, turning as if she knew he was out there, watching. Matthew suddenly felt like a voyeur. He looked away. "You cleared John Snow?"

"We did. He had nothing to do with Cam's murder."

"So he did lie about being in Indy? I wonder why?"

"Apparently his ex-wife hated him so much she didn't want him in Roberta's life. Father and daughter had been meeting without the wife's knowledge for weeks. Then when Roberta was killed he was reluctant for her to know because he thought she'd blame him somehow."

"That's ridiculous."

"Not entirely. Roberta's jogs were a ploy to meet with her father at the little diner down the road from the Quick Stop. In a way he was partly responsible. He'd insisted they keep their meetings secret."

Matthew shook his head. "The whole thing makes me sad."

"I know. John Snow's devastated by the loss of his daughter."

"Apparently he's not as uninterested as Leanne Snow believes."

"Apparently not."

Matthew frowned. "So why did Deets kill Roberta Snow and run my other applicants off?"

"I'm guessing he was afraid Cam's replacement would find the flash drive before he could. He was obviously pouring over Cam's computer and notes trying to figure out exactly what Cameron knew and where he might have stashed the information. After seeing what poor Cam went through, I'm amazed he didn't give the location of the flash drive up."

"Cam was much tougher than he looked."

"Obviously. Anyway, the real question is why didn't he take Alex out like he took out the others. He certainly had an opportunity."

"Alex is special. If this guy liked to collect one-of-a-kind people, she probably intrigued him. Besides, Alex figured out the clues Cam left us. She found the flash drive. If the killer was planning on making Alex part of his collection, it probably seemed easiest just to let her do his work for him and then bring her in."

"I'm sure he didn't count on her putting one over on him. It was pretty shrewd of her to switch out that flash drive."

"That's my girl. How's the case against Deets?"

"Strong, thanks to Alex. Cam's flash drive had actual video footage of Deets with two of the original victims. Cam had located some Mensa lectures where Deets scoped out his victims and he got access to the facilities' security tapes. That was pretty shrewd investigative work. We also found Cam's computer in Deets's house. And his textbooks. Along with an audio tape of you and Alex interviewing Leanne Snow."

"Really? Oh, the broken lamp. Deets must have bugged the house."

"It appears that way."

"Well, I'm glad Cam got his man."

"Yes. He did. I don't remember if I told you, Smart, I'm really sorry for your loss. Cam was a good man."

SMART ALEX

"He was. Thanks. Did Deets admit to paying Pence to rent the cars and follow Alex? Or threaten my applicants?"

"Not yet, but we brought Pence back in and paraded him past the Interview room and Deets reacted. I'm sure when I tell Deets Pence gave us his description he'll reconsider his silence. Oh, by the way, the lab found DNA evidence on the wig Alex pulled out of the canal and it implicates Deets too."

"It's all coming together."

"Yeah. I'm hoping his lawyer will help him see it's in his best legal interest to come clean and tell us everything. It might mean the difference between the death sentence and life in prison."

"Pardon me if I hope he doesn't come clean. If anybody deserves the death penalty it's this guy."

"Amen and amen."

"I've gotta go, Cindy. I'll talk to you soon."

Matthew picked up Max and climbed out of his car, locking it up. He wasn't entirely sure why he'd come to Alex's place after promising himself he'd give her some space. He just wanted to see her again. To make sure she was all right. And to determine if she was done with Smart Investigations, Inc. Though losing her as an assistant was a depressing thought, Matthew liked the possibilities her quitting would open up for them personally. If they weren't working together they'd be free to pursue a relationship.

Guilt blossomed with the thought. He couldn't stop thinking that Alex deserved so much more than to be unemployed with a boyfriend who would probably never deserve her.

He climbed the steps to her third floor apartment and lifted his hand, Max dancing around his feet. The door opened before he could knock and Alex stood there, looking flushed and sexy.

"Matthew. Hi."

Alex's voice was still husky from her bruised windpipe.

The thought brought guilt swimming back. She was supposed to be resting her voice. Another reason he shouldn't be there.

Max shot through the door, swiped his tongue over her bare foot and bolted to the couch. He jumped up, circled three times and plopped down with a sigh. Alex grinned. "I guess you're coming in."

Matthew frowned. "If you don't mind…"

She gave him a look and reached for his hand, pulling him through the door. "Don't be silly. Of course I don't mind. In fact, I'm glad you came by. I have something I need to talk to you about."

Matthew closed the door behind him, fighting panic. "Oh yeah? What's on your mind?"

"Come in and sit down. Would you like something to drink?"

Matthew shook his head. "I'm fine. Thanks." He watched her walk across the room toward the cluster of comfy looking furniture in front of a crackling fire. She wore short shorts that skimmed her curvy behind lovingly and didn't leave much to his imagination, and a tank top that emphasized her large breasts and narrow waist. She looked delicious and his jeans tightened at the sight. "Strange time of year for a fire," he said as he sat down next to Max.

She shrugged. "I know it's Spring but the nights are still cool." She dropped onto the couch next to him and turned, crossing her legs and dropping her arms over her knees. Despite his best intentions, Matthew pulled her vanilla sugar scent deep into his lungs on a long, slow intake of air. His jeans felt like they might cut him in half. "Besides, a fire comforts me."

He frowned. "You need comforting?"

Something heated slipped through her gaze and Matthew nearly groaned with need. It had been a huge mistake to come to her place. He started to stand. "I should get going. I just wanted to make sure you were okay."

She put a velvety soft hand on his arm to stop him. "Stay." She flushed as his gaze fixed on her hand and then skimmed upward, getting caught somewhere in the middle, where the hard buds of her nipples were clearly visible under the thin fabric of the tank top, before Matthew forced his gaze back to her face.

She wore the hint of a smile. "I'm tired of dancing around the elephant in the room."

Matthew swallowed hard. "Elephant?" He knew he sounded like an idiot, but her nearness was affecting him in ways he hadn't experienced for years. Since he'd been a randy teenager. "I don't understand."

"I think you do, Matthew." She leaned closer, her gaze filled with the burning need Matthew was feeling. "I've loved working with you at Smart Investigations…"

He frowned. Her use of past tense disturbed him. In that moment he realized he didn't want her to walk away. In any sense. "Alex, I—"

She put a finger on his lips, stopping him. "Let me say what I need to say."

He expelled air and nodded.

"I know you thought I was overqualified because of all my degrees but if I've learned anything over the years it's that those are just symbols and the stuff I learned to get them is nice but it's not horribly helpful in the real world. I believe everyone is born with a gift and I always thought my gift was my brains. I was wrong." She settled back against a couple of bright red throw pillows and smiled. "These last several days with you I learned that I haven't found my true gift yet. I think I know what it is, but it still needs to be honed. It needs to mature…to be framed. But more importantly, I learned that I no longer care what it is. I know what I want to do now and that's huge for me."

Because he couldn't help himself, he reached for her hand. "What do you want to do, Alex?" Some small, ridiculous part of him was praying she'd say, sleep with you Matthew. He nearly smiled at the thought.

"I want to work at Smart Investigations. I want to learn everything you can teach me about being a private investigator. And someday, I think I want to open my own agency."

He felt his eyes go wide. She'd caught him totally off guard. "I have to say I'm surprised. I'd thought after the week you had you'd run screaming from the job."

"Is that what you hoped I'd do?" she asked him with a frown.

Matthew leaned closer, rubbing her velvety hand in his. "Not by a long shot." He looked into her sexy eyes and tried to think of what he could say to let her know how he felt. It wasn't easy. Words weren't in any way adequate to the sentiment. Finally he just let the words free, trusting them to reflect his heart. "I want you working by my side for as long as you want to be there."

She blinked and then smiled. "Do you mean it?"

He lifted her hand and pressed a lingering kiss to her palm. "Yes. But if I'm being honest, some small part of me also hoped you'd want to walk away."

"But why?"

Matthew's gaze caught on her upper lip and he frowned. The slightly swollen wound that marred her perfect lip served as a reminder of a madman's obsession.

"Because I've wanted you since the moment you walked through my door." He captured her other hand and pulled them both up, kissing the back of first one and then the other. "I can't remember the last time a woman has affected me like you do, Alex. I'm totally smitten. I love the way you smell, the way you taste…" He glanced into her eyes and was charmed to see her flush, no doubt at the memory of their kiss. "I love to watch you walk. When you bite your lip I'm nearly undone. And if I could I'd watch you sleep for hours…maybe even days…on end."

Twin worry lines appeared between Alex's dark brows.

He realized he'd probably gone too far. Releasing her hands, Matthew offered her a sad smile. "I'm sorry. I didn't want to tell you because I knew it wasn't right. You deserve more than a man who can't stop thinking about having sex with you. You're way too smart and special for that." He stood. "I can't tell you how sorry I am, Alex. Of course I'll give you a strong letter of recommendation and I'll help you find a job at another agency if you'd like."

Alex surged to her feet and reached for him, her arms sliding around his neck. Before Matthew knew what she'd planned, Alex's satiny lips had descended on his. As she pressed her soft form close, Alex's entire body came alive, a coil of sizzling lust turning his gut to steel. Unable to resist what she offered, he wrapped his arms around her waist and tugged her close, deepening their kiss.

Alex made a soft sound of need against his mouth and her hands came up to slide through his hair. The feel of her strong fingers caressing his scalp and tangling in his hair nearly undid him.

Matthew forced himself to break the kiss before things spun out of control. She made a soft moue of regret as his lips left hers and pressed closer. "Alex, I…"

Her teeth captured his bottom lip and tugged in censure. "I want this, Matthew. I want us."

"But we can't work together."

Alex licked the spot where she'd bitten him and Matthew thought he might combust right on the spot. "Here's the deal. We'll take it slow. Pick our way carefully through the whole work and relationship thing. And we'll do it with the understanding that I'm going to be moving on someday. I was serious when I said I wanted my own agency. It's a long term goal but it's important to me."

"You deserve better than a boss who can't be in the same room with you without wanting to ravish you."

She waggled her eyebrows. "I deserve a man who wants exactly that. The boss part is temporary and I'm okay with it if you are." She frowned. "Look, Matthew,

I've been unhappy for a long time. I was unsure where I was going with my life and I didn't like any of my choices. Since I met you I discovered what I'm good at and what I want to do for the rest of my career. And I've found a man I want to do it with."

His expression must have shown his surprise at her words because she laughed, tapping him on the mouth with a velvety fingertip. "You didn't think you were the only one having these feelings did you?"

"I...guess I assumed I was."

"You know what they say about assuming?"

"Something about your ass. Which I'm very fond of by the way."

Alex's laugh was husky, filled with heat. "Your ass is pretty sexy too." To prove her point, she smacked him on both cheeks, squeezing them as she tugged him closer. "Now let's stop talking and get down to business." She grinned. "I believe you have some ravishing to do."


The End

# ABOUT THE AUTHOR

USA Today Bestselling Author Sam Cheever writes romantic paranormal/fantasy and mystery/suspense, creating stories that celebrate the joy of love in all its forms. Known for writing great characters, snappy dialogue, and unique and exhilarating stories, Sam is the award-winning author of 50+ books and has been writing for over a decade under several noms de plume.